After the way Max Heger had treated her, Selena didn't ever want to have anything to do with him again. But that was easier said than done, when he turned up, out of the blue, on her doorstep again. At least, she thought, it might give her an opportunity to be revenged on him! But things didn't work out exactly as Selena had planned.

THE LOVING SLAVE

Eighteen-year-old Gina had always hero-worshipped Quentin Hurst—but to him she was still just a child, and a tomboy at that. So she made a great effort and managed to turn herself into something more like a woman—and this time she began to feel he was returning her interest. But could she ever really compete with the elegant Blanche Edgar?

CAPTIVITY

To escape being married off to a rich man—*any* rich man!—by her snobbish and ambitious mother, Alex fled to Melbourne, only to meet someone who was just as determined as her mother had been. Chase Marshall offered her marriage as well—but Alex was under no illusions as to why: he simply thought she would be suitable. Well, he could keep his offer of marriage!

DARK SURRENDER

Was Brad Hewson interested in Julie or wasn't he? And while Julie was debating that question, it didn't help at all that she discovered that her stepfather was apparently embezzling from Brad and that somehow she would have to put that situation right. Yet more and more she was coming to realise that any woman who was foolish enough to love Brad was doomed to be hurt . . .

DECEPTION

Sick to death of being run after for her money, Thea ran away herself—to Drumlarig in the Scottish Highlands, where she had been happy when she was a child. But she only ran into more trouble, when she took a job as housekeeper to Logan Murray without telling him who she really was. And with Logan, a new set of problems developed . . .

COLLISION

BY

MARGARET PARGETER

MILLS & BOON LIMITED
15–16 BROOK'S MEWS
LONDON W1A 1DR

First published 1981
Australian copyright 1981
Philippine copyright 1981
This edition 1981

© Margaret Pargeter 1981

ISBN 0 263 73632 6

Set in Monophoto Times 10 on 10½ pt.

Made and printed in Great Britain by
Richard Clay (The Chaucer Press) Ltd,
Bungay, Suffolk

CHAPTER ONE

THE party was in full swing and the noise was terrible. Selena North sighed, wishing it was over, while fully aware that her opinion wouldn't be shared by the vast majority of her cousin's guests. She viewed them, the stars, or would-be stars, of the acting profession, her blue eyes too cynical for a girl of barely nineteen. They were mostly young people in their twenties and thirties, although some might not have been as old as herself. How eagerly they swarmed the huge lounge, their numbers steadily increasing with late arrivals until she thought the room, big though it was, would surely burst.

Clutching her soft drink tighter in her slim hands, she edged her way through the crowd, attempting to reach the adjoining balcony, which looked quieter. On her way there a half drunk youth laughingly grabbed her lemonade and after a disgusted sip, replaced it with a glass of whisky.

Dropping the lemonade on a nearby table, he grinned into her smooth young face. 'You won't get far on that, Selena darling.'

'Nobody was trying to,' she replied. She didn't like Primo Pleasure, with his silly talk and even sillier grin. She felt like telling him so, but she kept her wits about her. Evasive tactics, she had learnt since coming to live here, were often far more effective than head-on confrontations. Men like Primo were rarely got rid of by the latter.

'Can't you find me something to nibble, while you're at it?' she asked, masking her instinctive dislike with a sweetly innocent smile. 'I believe I saw some cheese straws over there a few minutes ago?'

While he went off obligingly after the cheese straws which had probably been eaten long ago, Selena continued on her way to the balcony. Here it was relatively peaceful and she was glad to escape, to relax for a few short moments and enjoy the wonderful view over the city. They were so high up that even at night the visual effect was extravagant, with millions of lights flung like a glittering tapestry, dramatically against the deep blue background of the sky.

Again she sighed, huddling closer against one of the marble pillars, trying to avoid the occasional probing glance of those who, like herself, had wandered outside. As she lived with Pearl she couldn't very well get out of attending the parties she gave, but this didn't mean she had to participate. Pearl only requested that she make herself generally useful, but as most of the refreshments were gone, apart from the drinks to which everyone appeared to be helping themselves, she was sure no one would miss her. If Pearl did miss her she would simply conclude that she had gone to bed. Pearl wouldn't worry. This evening she was too excited about the part she hoped to get in the latest Max Heger film to worry about anything else.

As another few people strolled out on to the balcony Selena wondered why anyone bothered to give such extravagant parties. Yet why shouldn't Pearl do as she pleased? When she was working she lived an almost frugal existence, up early and to bed early, sticking to a very strict routine. It was in between jobs that she believed in letting herself go, but this evening's effort, she had assured Selena, did have a practical purpose. Max Heger, the director, had said he might look in, and she was determined to use all her not inconsiderable charm if it would help her to get the contract she coveted.

She deserved to get it, too, Selena decided, staring reflectively down at the glass of unwanted whisky in her hand. It wasn't as if it had been the leading role. It was another part Pearl wanted, that of a very bitchy lady, a part she played with such natural talent that Selena couldn't think why Max Heger should hesitate. If this was what he was doing. She had never met him, but she had heard enough about him to realise he must know exactly what he was after. He didn't, apparently, know the meaning of uncertainty. If this was so then it looked as if he wasn't convinced Pearl was right for his next production, and if she didn't get the part she was going to be impossible to live with during the next few weeks.

Moodily Selena continued to stare out over night-time London, wishing she didn't have to live with Pearl another day. It could be several months, though, before her mother returned from abroad with her latest husband. In the meantime, she was stuck here with Pearl.

Unfortunately she wasn't earning enough to be completely independent, and the last time she had asked for help her mother had merely shaken her head and pleaded poverty. It had been the same when she was at school. She had usually had to do without the things which other girls had taken for granted. And, during school holidays, she had nearly always been palmed off on to Pearl or some other distant relative while her mother chose to be engaged in foreign parts.

On the other hand, her father, who lived in America with his second wife, was no better. Their indifference to what Selena privately termed their parental responsibilities had made her increasingly determined, over the years, to have nothing to do with the entertainment world when she grew up. It wasn't, she had decided bitterly, a good life at all. Apart from its being unreliable, career-wise, most of their friends were either divorced or separated or simply living together.

Pearl was luckier than most, for although her husband had just divorced her she usually had plenty of work, or offers of it. Strangely enough, she had nothing at the moment, or nothing, she said, worth considering. This made both her mood and temper uncertain. Selena was secretly praying that the famous Max Heger would waste no more time in giving Pearl exactly what she was after.

Frowning absently, Selena turned her fair head, as the tallness and breadth of the latest arrival on the balcony came between her and the scene she had been gazing at. Caught between the sudden change over from light to darkness, she was briefly blinded. When she blinked and looked again, it was to find her glance trapped by a pair of brilliant dark eyes. Apprehensively her own eyes widened until she was aware of nothing else, as she was caught, whipped up, devastated by a force of something almost dynamic. Frantically disbelieving, she clenched her tense fingers while her stunned mind hurtled backwards, refusing to halt.

It had happened over a week ago, when she had been late. Fervently hoping that her employer, Ronald Walker, whose latest manuscript she had been sent to type, on a temporary basis by the agency who employed her, would be late too, she hurried. Ronald, a university professor by day, was a writer at nights and weekends, which suited Selena very well as it enabled her to miss most of Pearl's friends, but if she didn't arrive at Ronald's house at the appointed hour he was inclined to fuss.

Selena grew even more agitated on discovering she must, in her haste, have pressed the wrong button on the lift. Instead of depositing her on the ground floor it had taken her below to the basement where penthouse owners, and sometimes their friends, garaged their cars. 'Blast!' she muttered, realising only as she stumbled out in the greeny light what had happened. She was so exasperated she stumbled again, so that the folder she carried dislodged itself from under her arm and bounced on to the concrete under a car. She got such a jolt she didn't see the man who had just left his car approaching, although the basement was quiet at this hour and there was no one else about.

Attempting to pick up the folder without actually

stopping, she crashed right into him and felt the impact of his tall, lean body run right through her.

In the semi-darkness their eyes met. It was merely a brief flicker of contact as her head jerked back from the broad crush of his chest, as impatiently he steadied the headlong rush of her impetuous limbs, but the effect was electric. They stared at each other while Selena sagged against him bewildered, entirely given up to new sensations. For a breathless, overwhelming moment, it seemed he was aware of what he was doing no more than she. Like two magnets drawn suddenly together, the space between them closed. Then his head bent and he kissed her, his mouth hard and cool on her startled, half parted lips. This, too, was as uncomfortable as the meeting of their eyes had been. There was no steady rise of pleasure, no enjoyable rising warmth. If there had been warmth at all, it changed instantly to a scorching fire—a fire which burnt, one which she felt spreading rapidly from her savagely crushed mouth to the innermost parts of her trembling body.

Yet her fundamental fear of it was such that it acted as an effective deterrent. Frantically she tried to escape the arms that tightened about her. She could feel herself growing giddy and had no wish to be trapped in the alien, violent world to which he seemed to be taking her. This wasn't real, it was a nightmare. As with a desperate effort she managed to release her bruised lips, the harsh rasping of his breath convinced her it was indeed.

So realistic was this impression that her imagination grew distorted and ran out of control. She began to believe he meant to do more than kiss her. The coldness of his eyes was aflame, as though he would have liked to possess her. Wildly she lashed out, catching the side of his hard brown face with a strength born of desperation.

With a harshly muttered oath he released her, but in doing so, as he stepped back, he seemed to lose his

balance. The last glimpse she had of him, he was stagger-
ing against a car, but she barely hesitated another
second. Her unconscious reflexes urged her to run and
instinctively she obeyed them. As she fled she told herself she hadn't hit him hard enough to justify his sharp
exclamation of pain.

All week she had hoped never to see him again,
making this her excuse for thinking of him constantly.
It took the noise of her glass hitting the marble slab at
her feet to bring her to her senses. Hastily gulping down
air into her depleted lungs, she bent automatically to
pick it up.

'Allow me.' Firmly, before she could touch it, the
man who had come between her and the lights, the man
who she was sure was the one who had kissed her in the
basement, held her back. Quickly he pushed the broken
glass out of sight with his foot, where it would be a
danger to nobody. There was a strong smell of whisky
and she saw his brows go up.

'I'm not usually so careless,' she stammered, half
stunned by suspicions that wouldn't go away.

Straightening his dark head, he stared at her coolly
again, a man she was sure she had never seen before,
but who continued to make her feel she was in the
middle of a bad dream. 'Perhaps you might be wiser to
stick to soft drinks in future. Whisky can't be the best
choice for a girl of your age.'

He thought she was drunk! The angry indignation
that swept through her did nothing to make her feel
better. About to defend herself fiercely against the cold
disapproval in his hard, handsome face, she hesitated.
Might it not be better to let him think she was a little
drunk than that he should suspect they had met before?
If they had met before. She couldn't be sure, and for a
crazy moment she thought she was going mad. He
might never have been near the basement and she
mustn't make a fool of herself by accusing him of
something he perhaps wasn't guilty of?

Yet that dark head seemed suddenly too familiar for comfort, the cool grey eyes too shrewdly narrowed on her hot, flushed face. Quickly, trying to appear indifferent, she said. 'A lot of girls drink whisky.'

'So I believe.' His slight shrug gave the impression he wasn't fully concentrating. Then, as his glance dropped to the shattered remains of her glass, he said. 'It's all right until you get to this stage.'

It took another deep breath to cool the impulse to defend herself. His voice was deep and charming, with just the merest hint of a drawl she couldn't place. She wished now that she had waited until the man, that night, had spoken, instead of fleeing at his first grunt of pain. A voice might be as hard to forget as a kiss but much easier to identify, and while a girl might ask a man to speak to her again she could never ask him to repeat the other. Her nerves tightening even to think of it, Selena looked at his mouth. It was a good mouth, the top lip firm and thin, the bottom one fuller, with just a hint of sensuousness. Dazedly she wondered about his age. He looked to be in his thirties and a man of some experience.

Hastily averting her curious gaze, she spoke quickly to cover her confusion, deciding to attack him, as he appeared to be attacking her. 'If you don't like it here you don't have to stay. I think you've probably gate-crashed, anyway?'

He lifted his hand briefly to rake back a lock of dark hair and she noticed, with a start, that his wrist was bandaged inside his cuff. 'What makes you think I wasn't invited?' he asked.

'Because I know most of Pearl's friends and I don't believe I've ever seen you.'

'I could be a new one.'

'Quite easily,' she conceded, hoping irrationally he wasn't. 'But if you were it's unlikely you'd be out here with me, Mr . . . er . . .?'

Leaning nearer, he coolly ignored her pointed prompt

over his name. 'I can assure you, miss, that I've known Miss Burnett for some considerable time, and if I'm not with her right now it could be because I caught a glimpse of an even more attractive young lady out here on the balcony.'

Selena's pulse rate quickened, she didn't know whether with anger or fright. He paid her compliments but didn't seem altogether sincere. He sounded slightly cynical, as if he had discovered an angel with feet of clay. Well, that might go for both of them! While in a mysterious way this stranger attracted her, all her instincts warned her against him.

'Don't tell me you've never been told you're attractive before?' he taunted, his brows faintly raised when she didn't reply.

Without any sense of being proud of herself, Selena knew she was reasonably good to look at, but she never considered herself beautiful. Her mirror informed her that she had heavy, tawny gold hair, that her face was delicately featured and she had wide, thickly lashed blue eyes. Her mirror also told her she was slim and graceful, but it didn't betray a certain sex appeal, so she had no idea about that. She only suspected she was attractive because one or two of Pearl's friends had hinted that they wouldn't mind having an affair with her, but she had never once thought of giving in to their demands. During the year she had lived here she had grown adept at avoiding the less desirable of Pearl's men friends.

As her companion's impatience of her prolonged silence became obvious, she retorted rather sharply, 'If you know anything at all about Pearl's circle, you must know that compliments like that are two a penny and usually meaningless. I rarely take them seriously.'

This time when his brows rose, he looked amused. 'You seem to imply that Pearl's way of life is superficial.'

'Isn't it?' She wished she could look him straight in the face as she challenged him, but she couldn't risk that cool dark gaze too often, not until she could be assured of her own composure. Settling for the top button of his shirt, she declared sweepingly, 'Acting must be artificial, creating something which doesn't really exist. It's like living in a dream world.'

'One shared by most artists,' he agreed dryly. 'But where would we be without them? Can you imagine a world without entertainment, something which has existed since the beginning of time? Sometimes,' he added soberly, 'it's better to give people a little of what they fancy, which doesn't necessarily mean an overdose of sex or pornography.'

Feeling suitably chastised didn't prove she was wholly convinced, or that she was going to apologise! Selena was only too conscious that his smile gave the impression that he was soothing a capricious child. 'Perhaps you're right,' she admitted distantly. 'Now, if you'll excuse me . . .' Determinedly she turned away. One couldn't very well go on addressing a top button, not even if one wanted to.

As she made to pass, he caught her arm. 'Come and have supper with me. I'd like to talk to you.'

'What? Now?' Surprise made her unwary enough to raise startled eyes to his and again she was caught in that curious trap of the senses. For a long moment, as a peculiar kind of tension beamed between them, neither of them moved. The man was the first to recover his equilibrium.

'Why not?' he asked lightly. 'The night's still young.'

'Actually,' she muttered, her mind still dazed in confusion, 'I was thinking of bed.'

'I wouldn't mind that myself,' he said sardonically, 'but I prefer more privacy. This place is rather crowded.'

Startled, she stared at him. He didn't know she lived here and must have misconstrued what she had said. Or pretended to. Another disquieting thought struck her, causing her cheeks to go pink with embarrassment. If he had mistaken her innocent remark for something else, it could mean he was used to girls of her age making outrageous suggestions.

A biting retort rose to her lips, but before she could utter it he continued, 'Go and find your coat, if you brought one. We can save the bedroom scene for later. You're a bit young to be in such a hurry, but keep it in mind. If you're interested, it's fixed in mine—and underlined.'

He was insulting, even allowing for the fact that he might have got the wrong impression. She would be a fool to go anywhere with him! It made her even more furious, therefore, to hear herself agreeing to collect her wrap on the way out.

'Meet me at the door, then, in five minutes,' he commanded, not seeming in the least surprised by such instant capitulation. 'I want a word with Miss Burnett if possible, before I leave.'

If Selena had harboured any doubts about his knowing Pearl, they were dispelled by the warm smile on Pearl's face when she glanced up to find him standing beside her. Diving in the opposite direction, Selena was slightly shattered by an enormous surge of relief.

But in spite of this, as she waited outside, she wondered if she were being sensible. This was the first date of this kind she had ever made and her doubts about it were increasing rapidly. This man, who she felt uneasily deliberately avoided giving his name, was older than herself. He couldn't be less than in his thirties, and had obviously been around. He possessed the kind of arrogant confidence which seemed a clear indication of the kind of life he led.

A trifle apprehensively, Selena drew her short fur jacket closer around her. She must have been crazy to agree to going anywhere with him, yet, funnily enough, she felt she could trust him. And she wouldn't stay out long, no longer than an hour. Firmly she put from her mind his comments about taking her to bed. Most of

Pearl's friends occasionally said shocking things, but often, Selena suspected, merely for effect.

Her thoughts returning to Pearl, Selena frowned. Perhaps she should have told her she was going out, but she would probably be home again before Pearl missed her. If Pearl ever gave her another thought before morning. Midday would probably find Pearl still in bed, complaining of a foul headache. Or again, if Max Heger did turn up with a contract, she could be in the best of moods.

The man, as Selena now called him, soon followed her. Abruptly breaking through a group of young people who tried to delay him in the doorway, he joined her in such a way that it would have been difficult to decide that they were leaving together. In the lift she didn't speak, nor did he. He seemed content to watch her broodingly, the intentness of his gaze being the only expression on his otherwise inscrutable face.

It was only as he settled beside her in the back of the taxi he hailed that he asked casually, 'Aren't you nervous of my intentions?'

'Should I be?' She hoped her careless shrug hid her growing sense of danger.

'Not really,' he allowed, yet his low laughter was oddly taunting, 'but I shouldn't have thought you were that confident.'

Stung, she sat upright. 'You asked me out,' she replied angrily. 'If it was just for the pleasure of insulting me then you'd better drop me off at once.'

'I don't happen to want to.' His voice was silky, but his hand curved around her arm forcibly, as if to make sure she didn't try and jump out.

'It's all so silly!' she protested, her blue eyes incredulous, as she became fully aware of what she was doing, 'Please,' she pleaded, 'take me back.'

'Too late,' he grunted derisively. 'You should have had second thoughts before we left. You should have realised then that I'm a bit out of your league.'

She stared at him, seeing the mocking, amused quirk on his mouth. Furious, because he was so right, she accused him, 'You didn't give me a chance!'

Her indignation didn't appear to impress him. 'Do you always make dates with strange men so easily?' he asked.

He sounded so cynical she was compelled to exclaim. 'Why bother with me if you disapprove of me so much?'

'Touché,' he smiled grimly. 'Perhaps I was testing you. Maybe I was hoping you would refuse to have anything to do with me.'

A faint colour touched her lovely cheekbones. 'Then you were caught in your own trap. Now you find you're obliged to buy me my supper.'

'And dance with you, perhaps?'

Nervously she tried to wrest her arm from the disturbing grip of his fingers. 'You said nothing about that!'

'I took it for granted, as you were so co-operative about everything else.'

Because this seemed to imply that she was the sort of girl who was game for anything, Selena almost shivered with humiliation. Weakly she swallowed. 'I don't usually go out with a man unless we've been properly introduced.'

'I should hope not!'

She was surprised that his face was suddenly grim, and she muttered ungraciously, 'You're the one who's making it all sound so outrageous. You said you knew Pearl and I agreed to come out with you for—well, for a drink or something. What's there to make such a fuss about in that?'

For a second he looked mildly explosive, then a flicker of humour returned to his hard face. 'You're right, of course. I think it was meeting the way we did that threw me. I never believed it could happen.'

This time Selena had to swallow twice and turn away

from him, lest her face gave her away. 'What do you mean?'

'I'm talking about a little spark of electricity,' he said, looking straight ahead.

Instantly wary, Selena felt her nerves tighten and wished she didn't remember it too. Of course he might only be thinking of this evening on the balcony, for he couldn't be sure they had met before. Neither could she. 'The sort of thing you're talking about only exists in story books,' she said emphatically.

'The idea must have come from somewhere,' he replied thoughtfully.

'I expect from someone's imagination,' she murmured, wondering why her pulse was suddenly racing?

Briefly his fingers lingered on it with an odd satisfaction, then wryly he smiled. 'You certainly know how to subdue any man's imagination.'

'Perhaps you should be grateful.'

'Perhaps I am,' he smiled. 'My life's difficult enough without looking for more complications.'

Selena was thankful she was in no way able to reply to that, but she couldn't help wondering if the complications he mentioned were feminine. Then, to her relief, they arrived at their destination. It was a nightclub, one she had never been to before. It was high up on the rooftops and was called the Pink Lagoon.

'Why pink?' she asked, attempting to hide her foolishly increasing uncertainty, as they were seated. 'I've never heard of a pink lagoon.'

'I know one.' He was studying her keenly across the secluded table he had procured with astonishing ease in a room already crowded. 'At least, it's pink at certain times. At dawn, mostly, or so it seems to me. I'll take you and show you one day, if you like.'

'I'll take your word for it,' she assured him hastily, then asked in confusion, 'Why dawn? Couldn't you sleep?'

'Perhaps,' he teased lightly, 'I had no one to keep me in bed.'

Warmth such as she had never experienced before until this moment flooded her body as he continued to stare at her closely. It wasn't until she felt she was drowning in the glittering depth of his eyes that she managed to wrench hers away. She might have known he would say something like that. He had asked her out, yet seemed determined to shake her, and, because she was reacting so sensitively to almost everything he said, he must be deriving a great deal of satisfaction.

This time, without waiting for her comment, he beckoned to the hovering waiter. Without consulting her he ordered from an extensive menu, but while his arrogant presumption made her quiver, she didn't say anything. She was somehow too shaken by her own rash conduct in coming here this evening to even think of criticising anything he did.

When they were alone again he said, 'Don't you think it might be a good idea if we introduced ourselves?'

'I suppose so,' she agreed, a little desperately, not being at all sure now that she really wanted to know his name. Such an attitude, she realised, must be slightly ridiculous, but after this evening it was unlikely she would ever see him again.

'You don't seem to share my enthusiasm,' he taunted softly. 'Which surprises me, when you've been curious for so long.'

'I guessed you're an actor.' Momentarily her blue eyes were as intent as his. Carefully she studied his face, the hard, classical lines of it, suddenly lost in it. He had what she called a stubborn chin, jutting with a deep cleft in it. His mouth was strong, his nose straight, while his eyes, almost as thickly fringed as her own, had a directness which she found disconcerting. His hair, waving slightly, dark and crisp, made her tremble with an illogical desire to run her fingers through it, a desire she had never felt before with any other man. Like her sudden disinclination to know his name, this didn't seem to make sense, either. 'I feel,' she frowned, 'I should remember. Your face seems vaguely familiar, but I don't see many films.'

His brows rose wryly. 'You really don't care for the acting profession, do you?'

Stiffly she replied, 'I've lived with people who've had to do with it all my life.'

'Which explains everything?'

Indignant of his irony, she retorted, 'A few get away with it, but a lot don't.'

'It can be very rewarding.'

'Financially, you mean?'

'Most people,' he remarked dryly, 'consider their careers from that point of view.'

'There's job satisfaction?'

'That, too.'

'But what about their private lives?' she came back to what she considered was the more important. 'Actors work hard, yet their personal lives are often a mess.'

'Strong words?' he teased lightly.

It annoyed her, suddenly out of all proportion, that he didn't appear to be taking her seriously, yet she was startled to hear herself daring to ask, 'How many wives do you have scattered around? How many children suffering because of your broken marriages?'

Knowing she had overstepped the mark, she felt a swift apprehension as his eyes glittered with anger. Then, as though a shutter had come down, his face was expressionless again. 'You appear convinced that broken marriages are the prerogative of the film industry, but, to satisfy your curiosity, I've never had a divorce, and, as far as I know, no children. I've had one wife, but she died ten years ago.'

Immediately Selena felt ashamed, then her face set stubbornly. He was just waiting for her to begin sympathising, then he would snub her unmercifully yet again. She did feel, though, that she owed him some sort of apology. 'I'm sorry, that was inexcusable of me.

Your private affairs are none of my business.'

'Hmm.' His mouth quirked, but she couldn't believe it was with amusement. 'You're too impulsive, but perhaps I'd rather have your interest than indifference.'

Her heart, not reassured, beat faster. There was something vaguely unsettling in his voice which again prompted her to speak without thinking. 'I'm not interested in you particularly, Mr ... er ...'

'But I'm hoping you're going to be.' His voice, still gentle, contained an element of something very like a threat. 'In the meantime,' he went on, without giving her a chance to deny it, 'I think we'll return to formalities. You can't call me Mr Er indefinitely.'

'No,' she agreed in some confusion. 'My name's Selena North.'

'And mine's Max Heger.'

'Max Heger!' If he had dropped a bomb she couldn't have received a greater shock. Entirely stunned, her startled eyes flew to his, but she could read nothing in them to convince her he was joking. 'You can't be!' she breathed.

'You could always check?' he suggested, unperturbed.

Swiftly, as a choking panic rose within her, Selena jumped to her feet. She would have fled but for his quick grasp on her wrist.

'Do you always run away?' he snapped, with more than a hint of impatience.

Was he referring to their previous meeting? Did he know? Was he the man in the basement? Unhappily aware of the times she had asked herself these questions, Selena thrust her suspicions aside. He might only be passing an idle remark. Even so, her breath was still short as she exclaimed, 'I think, tonight, I have good reason.'

'You have?'

Hating the flicker of amusement in his eyes, she counted ten before trying to be as devious herself. 'You should have told me as soon as we met that you were

Max Heger, the famous director.'

'Ah,' he replied ruefully. 'Maybe I wasn't given the opportunity.'

Again she was sure there was more to what he said than was immediately apparent. 'I don't like being made a fool of, Mr Heger,' she retorted sharply. 'Now that you've told me, I can't understand why I didn't recognise your face, but that doesn't excuse you. I think you deliberately took advantage of me.'

'Oh, come,' he smiled, this time more soothingly, 'I wasn't even trying to make a fool of you. And do sit down. People are beginning to look curious, and I'm not after extra publicity.'

'Really?' Her wayward lips curled tauntingly. 'I thought men in your position thrived on it?'

'You're a little cat, aren't you?' he drawled mildly. 'You're inclined to spit at the least thing and your claws are too sharp by far.'

'You deceived me.' Reluctantly she slid back into her chair. 'Don't you agree I've a right to be angry?'

His grey eyes held hers cynically. 'No, I don't. I'm not even convinced you didn't know who I was all the time.'

'How could I?' she countered, enraged.

'Quite easily,' he returned crisply.

Uneasily she hesitated, knowing this was true. He was very well known, his name a byword in the film industry and other, related ones. His face ought to have been instantly recognisable, even though she rarely glanced at the numerous cuttings Pearl kept. 'I'm sorry,' she murmured tensely, 'if I haven't noticed things I should have.'

'Never mind,' he said smoothly, in what she was coming to think of as his normal mocking tones. 'If you haven't noticed me in the past, I'll have to make sure you do in future.'

'In future?' she repeated, frowning as this reminded her of something. Anxiously her thoughts raced ahead, concentrating on Pearl now, rather than herself. 'The part Pearl would like in your new film?' she asked breathlessly, 'Has she got it?'

'So,' he said sharply, 'you know about that?'

Selena's glance wavered, dropping to the dim light on the table. Perhaps she shouldn't have mentioned this to Max Heger. It mightn't help Pearl much if he was to think she was complaining about having to wait. 'I know she's been hoping to hear something,' she replied cautiously.

His voice was faintly cynical. 'So do I.'

'Do you enjoy keeping people in suspense?' she demanded coldly, caution forgotten, infuriated by his apparent indifference.

He surveyed her calmly for a long, silent moment. 'As a matter of fact,' he said at last, 'I was on my way to see her about a week ago when I met with a slight accident.'

'An accident?' Selena echoed weakly.

'Yes.' His voice was silky while his eyes left hers to rest speculatively on his bandaged wrist. 'I cracked a bone and had to have it fixed. After which I had another appointment, which left me with no more time to see Pearl that evening.'

'I see.' Selena felt a shiver run right through her.

This time his voice was very smooth indeed. 'I was hoping,' he said, 'that you might.'

CHAPTER TWO

FEELING painfully unsure of herself, Selena murmured, 'I'm sorry about your wrist.'

'I'm sure you are.'

Deciding to ignore the obvious irony—and the heat in her cheeks—she continued bravely, 'When you said you wanted a word with Pearl before we left, I just wondered, that's all.'

His broad shoulders moved slightly. 'A party is scarcely the place for a serious discussion. I'm seeing her in the morning.'

Pearl would be pleased about that. She would be in a good mood. Unless—? Her blue eyes dark with dismay, Selena looked across at Max Heger. 'Did you mention me?'

'No,' his brows rose derisively. 'How could I when I didn't even know your name?' Then, dismissing Pearl abruptly, he came around the table and drew Selena firmly to her feet. 'Come on, let's dance. We can forget the more serious side of life for a change.'

He was an excellent dancer and so was Selena, usually. Her limbs were young and supple and she was naturally responsive to rhythm of any kind. Yet tonight, dancing with Max Heger, she was afraid to let herself go. When he held her close she grew curiously weak, and when his arms tightened she felt dizzy as a kind of passionate excitement began flickering through her. With a frightening certainty she knew she had been in this man's arms before.

But when she gasped and pulled away, he didn't attempt to stop her. He merely sighed and said, 'We'd better retire. I appear to be having a peculiar effect on you and I don't enjoy dancing with stiff little boards.'

23

Mortified, she didn't attempt to explain what didn't make sense, not even to herself. He called her a stiff little board, while inside she trembled.

'We'll have a last drink then I'll take you home,' he glanced at her enquiringly, 'wherever that may be?'

Evading a direct reply, she sat down again rather helplessly. She didn't want another drink, but neither did she want him to know where she lived. She was sure that after this evening she would be wiser not to see him again, and, if he were to discover she lived with Pearl, he might ask her to. It was a risk Selena preferred not to take. If she was clever she might, in a few minutes, manage to evade him and go home by herself.

Yet before she had time to think of anything he had reached for her hand. Holding it tightly, so she couldn't escape him, he spoke firmly, clearly guessing her intentions. 'Why is it you always want to run away from me, Selena? I don't want you rushing off. I'd like you to stay and tell me about yourself.'

Her fingers tense within his warm clasp, her startled eyes flew to his. His cool grey glance narrowed on her grimly, sending a curious tremor running right down through her. It seemed to warn her again to be careful.

'There's nothing much to tell.' She made an effort to speak lightly.

'Because you're so young, you mean?'

'I'm not that young.' She paused, aware he was about to ask. 'I was nineteen a week ago.'

'A week ago?'

'Yes.' She didn't know what else to say and had no idea why he frowned.

'You had a party, of course?'

'No. My parents are abroad,' again she anticipated his query, without providing details.

'I expect you had some sort of celebration, though? I suppose you have plenty of boy-friends?'

'Oh, I have lots,' she agreed, and wondered why she had bothered to lie when she saw his face darken.

He appeared displeased, but when she feared he was about to pursue the subject he surprised her by changing it abruptly. 'How do you come to know Pearl Burnett?'

This was a question Selena had hoped he wouldn't ask, and now that he had she saw no way of evading an answer. It would be foolish to pretend that Pearl was merely a passing acquaintance, and not very sensible either. It wasn't that she was ashamed of claiming a relationship with Pearl, who was a well known and popular actress. It just seemed to Selena that the less Max Heger knew about her the better. Then, with a sigh, she realised she could be devious with a man like this only up to a point, and having been foolish enough to come out with him she might be equally foolish to jib at the consequences.

Reluctantly she enlightened him, 'Pearl is a distant relation of my mother's, and I live with her.'

'You live with her? I see . . .'

Selena noticed his mouth tighten, as though he saw a lot of things he didn't really like. It was obvious that he imagined she led a very gay life and, because of it, was far from as innocent as she looked. At the same time, in spite of the cynicism he displayed, he appeared slightly more relaxed.

Studying her carefully, he remarked, 'I can't remember seeing you in anything.'

'I'm not an actress, if that's what you mean,' she assured him hastily. 'Nor would I want to be.'

Her slightly contemptuous tones were ignored this time. 'What do you do, then?'

Suddenly she was cautious. Whatever happened, he mustn't connect her with the folder that had fallen under the car, and to mention she was a typist might easily betray her. 'I do nothing very much,' she hedged.

His eyes, still fixed on her closely, narrowed with scepticism. 'Why are you doing—nothing much?'

'Why not?' she shrugged, hoping to give the impression that she wasn't ashamed of being idle. He wasn't easy to deceive, and while she wasn't proud of herself for doing it she defended herself defiantly. There was no reason why she should tell Max Heger anything, none whatsoever. He couldn't be genuinely interested anyway.

As though her deliberate prevarication annoyed him he made no further comment. Instead he sat silent for a few seconds, still surveying her, then said abruptly, 'I think we'll get out of here.'

Having expected to be taken straight back to Pearl's penthouse, Selena was startled to find they were going in another direction. They were still in the West End, she wasn't sure where as it was raining heavily, but she fancied it was in the region of Hyde Park. While she was debating as to the wisdom of asking if there had been some mistake, the taxi drew up outside a tall house in a quiet corner. Before she could protest Max Heger had paid the man and they were standing on the wet pavement.

Taking hold of her arm, he turned her firmly towards the house, only pausing when she said coldly, 'This isn't where I live.'

'I'm not pretending it is,' he retorted curtly, through the darkness meeting her apprehensive eyes. 'Nor am I asking you to move in with me. The worst I have in mind this evening is a cup of coffee. If you had lived with your parents, I would probably have taken you back to their place and begged one from you.'

Because he could have coffee without her being there, she hesitated reluctantly, far from convinced that, in bringing her here, he had had coffee on his mind at all. 'It's getting late,' she glanced at his watchful face doubtfully, 'I have to get home yet.'

'After we have coffee,' he said smoothly, 'I'll ring for another taxi. I'm afraid I won't be able to drive my own car for another day or two, not until my wrist recovers, but I'm quite able to see you home.'

His establishment did nothing to settle her growing unease. Never having been a girl for acting out of character, she found it more difficult than she had anticipated. Because she had always considered her family had too little regard for the ordinary conventions, she had, almost fanatically, tried to stick to them herself. She might, she realised, have grown oversensitive, but there seemed nothing she could do about it. And such a code of behaviour, she was discovering, wasn't something which could be cast aside in the matter of minutes, not even for a man as charmingly formidable as Max Heger.

Inside his house, where she suddenly found herself without quite realising how she got there, she wondered, with despair, how she could have allowed herself to be so easily persuaded. She had protested but even she could recognise a feeble effort. And while she could only suppose that some kind of regrettable curiosity was responsible, she was vaguely aware she might be stepping straight into danger. Men didn't always respect girls who visited their homes at midnight.

The spacious hall, covered by a thick offwhite carpet, was offset by pale blue walls and dark panelling, the whole beautifully embellished by colourful, impressive paintings and other imposing pieces of valuable decor. It was an entrance which seemed to give an immediate indication of its owner's personality. Nothing obtruded, yet one was at once completely aware of everything.

Again Selena shivered as, without pausing, Max Heger guided her up a wide staircase to the first floor. Passing several doors, he pushed open one leading to a small sitting-room. The cosiness of it surprised her and he noticed.

'I thought you might like this better than the larger lounge next door. I usually use this one when I'm on my own.'

Strangely enough, this only served to increase Selena's pulse rate, yet she found herself regarding the book-lined walls, the comfortable chairs and long settee with approval. Pearl's penthouse might be smart, but it lacked the homeliness which, to a certain extent, this house possessed.'

'Sit down, won't you.' Max Heger's eyes rested on her expressive face with a flicker of amusement. 'It won't take me a moment to make coffee.'

It reassured her a little more to know he did, in spite of her former misgivings, intend making some. 'Have you lived here long?' she asked, smiling at him impulsively.

Her smile, the way it lit up her whole face, appeared to startle him briefly. 'Some years,' he answered slowly, as her smile faded. 'I'm abroad a lot, so I'm afraid it's unoccupied for long periods. I find it useful while I'm in London.'

'So you might be off again soon?'

'Don't bank on it,' he replied.

His dry observation, seeming to shift, as it did, their relationship to a more personal level, made her shiver. 'It didn't even occur to me,' she denied swiftly.

'I'd take some convincing of that,' he mocked softly.

All of a sudden her heart was beating too heavily. She felt tired and overwrought, almost to the point of tears. She had just arrived, yet she knew an urgent desire to escape.

'If you must make coffee, then I'd be grateful if you made it straight away,' she said stiffly, 'then I can go home. Pearl will be worried.'

'Will she?' This time sarcasm edged his deep voice, as if he was extremely sceptical. 'Well, sit down,' he relented, when Selena didn't reply, 'while I see what I can find in the kitchen.'

As the heating was on, Selena discarded her fur jacket and sat carefully on the settee. There were books on two of the armchairs, a pile of papers on the third, but there was nothing on the settee except several large cushions. Sinking into them, she sighed as the peace of the room gently soothed her. If only Pearl had a room like this how easy it would be to relax, but Pearl favoured black and white with brilliant splashes of purple, yellow and scarlet, and a square-cut design to everything, even the curtains. But then Pearl liked her decor ultra-modern and smart. She had no time for anything remotely sentimental. Cabbage roses and country gardens rambling over chintzy covers definitely weren't her thing.

After he had promised that he wouldn't be a moment, it surprised Selena when Max Heger didn't return almost immediately with their coffee. By the time he did she was fast asleep.

Perhaps because she was young and tired, she slept soundly, and had no idea what woke her up. Nor, when she did so, could she think where she was. She was only conscious of a terrible feeling of dread. When, a second later, she fully recovered her senses she was horrified. She was still lying on the settee, warm and comfortable, but with Max Heger stretched out now beside her, his arm around her, and, owing to the narrowness of their bed, half on top of her, his tall body heavy on hers. As her eyes widened, in a kind of wild apprehension she noticed daylight stealing in through the window.

Suddenly, frantically, she tried to twist upright away from him, but the strong arm which encircled her refused to let her go. Trembling with a growing terror, she paused to draw an unsteady breath. How long had they lain here asleep? And Max Heger appeared to have slept long and deeply. In stunned amazement her glance flickered over his face. A lot of the lines were gone from his broad, intelligent forehead and around his eyes, while his firm mouth was relaxed and softer. To her fury, Selena thought she could even detect a faint smile.

Yet, about to make another, more determined attempt to escape, she found herself hesitating shamefully. Staring at his mouth, she felt a strange urge to touch it, to trace its arrogant shape with her fingers, to even place her own mouth against it. Then, as if this wasn't enough, the unconscious attraction she felt for Max Heger threatened to take over completely. Helplessly, as though possessed by previously dormant instincts, her gaze travelled over him, coming to rest on the open front of his shirt. His chest was covered with thick, dark hair, as he drew a sudden deep breath the muscles rippled under smooth skin. Again Selena felt the force of a regrettable desire to touch him. For all he hadn't an ounce of surplus fat on him he had a strong, very sensuous body. This she recognised, and her own softer, feminine one reacted disconcertingly. In a confused daze she gasped, quite unable to control the feelings which suddenly swept through her. The weight of his limbs, especially, seemed to be tormenting her.

In a trance, her eyes returned to his face, to find him awake and staring at her cryptically. Something in his eyes looked very like flames and frightened her. Brought abruptly to her senses, she began to struggle. Hot with humiliation, she exclaimed, 'I don't know if this is your idea of a joke, but it isn't mine!'

'Nor mine, actually,' he replied curtly.

'Well, let me go, then!' she cried, her panic increasing rapidly as he made no attempt to move.

'In a minute,' he murmured softly.

'In a minute?' Rage making her heart beat furiously, she was forced to stop struggling in order to find her breath. If she could she would have drawn her nails down his mocking face, but, as if he guessed what was on her mind, his arms tightened until she was all but helpless.

'This is ridiculous!' she panted. 'Let me go, Max, at once!'

'Not yet.'

The hardness of his voice brought quick tears to her eyes. She tried to blink them away. 'You had no right to do this to me!'

'You fell asleep on your own accord,' he pointed out

coolly, 'I didn't ask you to do that.'

'You could have woken me up,' she retorted sharply. 'I was tired.'

'You were?' he taunted, staring indifferently into her drenched eyes. 'I wonder what with—if you have no job? Too many late nights, most probably. It can't be pushing all the labour-saving buttons in Pearl's flat.'

'Just what are you insinuating?' she whispered fiercely, realising their breath was intermingling in the most disturbing way. His face only an inch or so away from her own, and the scent of his skin, was bothering her intensely.

'Do I have to spell it out?' he grated, his lips twisting. 'Too many drinks of the wrong kind. Too many boy-friends of the wrong kind, too. I happened to see the specimen who was supplying you with whisky.'

'You're beyond a joke!' she gasped, denying nothing.

'Aren't I right, though?'

'No!' The outraged jerk which accompanied her ex-clamation brought her too near and she pressed back as far as she was able. 'Oh, why,' she moaned, 'are you keeping me here? What will people think? It's not as if I've done anything to deserve it. Unless . . .' Bewildered, she heard her voice trailing off and found herself staring at his bandaged wrist, as he brushed a tumbled lock of tawny hair from her brow. 'Oh, dear,' she gulped, tears of self-pity running over the guilty heat in her cheeks on to her mouth.

'Exactly,' he said softly, rubbing the tear from her tremulous lips with a careful finger, then, to her dismay, as another one rolled to join it, brushing this one away with his mouth.

'No!' she cried again, which was a mistake as it parted her lips in a most provoking manner.

With a thick groan, Max Heger tightened his arms about her while his mouth crushed hers, like a flower might be crushed by a ruthless predator. Selena felt pain—pain from his mouth and the savage weight of his pressing limbs, but it was a hurt like none other. Mixed with a burning fire, it swept right through her, drowning all reason. With a frantic strength she freed her arms to cling to him blindly, uncaring that he was pressing her into the settee with total abandonment.

It was a shock to hear him speak, for she was still hurtling towards the stars, completely at the mercy of her spinning senses. When his mouth eased reluctantly from her own, she wanted to protest.

As though he guessed this, he kissed her again, but this time lightly. 'This is something we do rather well together, isn't it?'

'I . . .' Momentarily her voice wouldn't come and she had to give up. Her heart seemed somewhere in her throat, preventing articulation.

'You were the girl in the basement, the one I have to thank for my fractured wrist, aren't you?'

'Yes.' She seemed beyond deviation.

'Why are you so sure?' his voice changed silkily.

Desperately Selena tried to gather her scattered wits before another equally foolish confession escaped her. 'I think I remember you,' she managed vaguely, as if it were quite possible she could be mistaken.

'You know damn well you do!' Suddenly he shifted his weight, easing himself slowly from her, leaving her prey to a strange mixture of relief and regret. 'And you know which part of you can't forget.'

Her heart racing out of control, Selena pulled herself up with difficulty, noting bitterly that he made no attempt to help her. Still feeling unsteady, she succeeded in getting to her feet. Outside it was dawn and she turned to Max Heger, accusing him wildly. 'Why did you bring me here and deliberately try to keep me all night? Whatever will people think?'

'That appears to be your main worry.'

His face was pale but quite hard. He's like a piece of stone, she thought, distraught. Defiantly she said. 'Why shouldn't it be? Just because you have no regard for public opinion it doesn't mean everyone else likes to ignore it too.'

'Was it my fault you fell asleep?' he asked coldly.

'No!' she almost shouted from sheer agitation. 'But you could have woken me up, you didn't have to go to sleep as well.'

'I didn't intend to sleep, either.' His mouth went wry, as if he doubted she would believe him. 'I tried to wake you, but you were dead to the world, and that was where I obviously made a mistake. I decided to let you rest for ten minutes and must have dozed off myself.'

Vividly she coloured. 'You were stretched out beside me!'

'Perhaps that just happened, too,' he rejoined sardonically. 'It could be that my body was more immediately ambitious than my mind. I always thought my mind was in control, but now I'm not so sure.'

'I'd take a lot of convincing of that,' she replied sceptically.

His mouth compressed to a hard line as he stared at her. 'I'm beginning to think you'd take a lot of convincing about anything. For one so young you're far too cynical.'

Somehow that hurt, although she wasn't sure why. Angry, because he had the ability to wound her, she said sharply, 'Well, you've gained nothing by bringing me here tonight.'

'I didn't actually hope to gain anything,' he stated grimly. 'I simply wanted to satisfy my curiosity.'

Startled, she blinked at him. 'If you were curious about something why didn't you ask me at the Pink Lagoon?'

Like a hawk he came back, his eyes glinting, 'I brought you here as it was the only way I could know for sure. If I'd asked you if you were the girl I'd kissed below Pearl's flat, you would have denied it. Or again, if you'd blushed and agreed, it wouldn't have been the first time a girl had jumped at the chance of getting to know me, regardless of the truth.'

Feeling terribly on her guard all of a sudden, Selena shook her head. Uncertain as to what he was getting at, she mistrusted the gleam in his eye. 'I don't know what conclusions you've come to about me, Mr Heger, but I'd rather you didn't tell me. All I'm interested in at the moment is getting home.'

'You think I'm outrageous because I wanted to discover if you were the girl who'd put me out of action for a week?'

'Only your method of going about it, perhaps.'

'But I only hurt your pride, while you resorted to physical violence.'

'I refuse to believe——' she began, then paused to frown as her glance jumped to his injured wrist, 'At least, I didn't mean to push you, and I'm sorry if it's caused you some inconvenience, but you gave me a fright.'

'Was that all?'

'What more could there be?'

His eyes narrowed, a flame flaring in the depth of the clear grey, to be as swiftly subdued as she flinched apprehensively. 'I hope to heaven you're right! You intrigued me, stirred my imagination, but my schedule is too full to allow for anything else at the moment. Now I'll take you home, to your proper bed.'

As she stared at him, not knowing what to make of his harsh exclamation, she saw his nostrils flare with a tight impatience as he turned and picked up her jacket.

'You'd better put this on,' he held it open. 'The morning air will be cold.'

'Oh, yes.' Blindly Selena slipped her arms into it. 'It belongs to Pearl and I shouldn't like to lose it.'

'Haven't you one of your own?'

'Not yet, but I don't mind. It's Pearl who insists I use this.'

He made no comment, other than to glance at her closely again as they left, and had little more to say until they arrived at the flat. Briefly, as she thanked him stiffly for bringing her home, he said, 'I'll be back in a few hours' time to see Pearl and I'd like you to be there as well.'

In spite of another quick surge of the anger this man could so easily provoke, her voice held a note of pleading disbelief. 'Is that a threat or a request, Mr Heger, or are you just trying to be polite?'

'Either of the first two will do,' he replied smoothly, 'just as long as you turn up. Women are notoriously unpredictable. And the name's Max.'

Not trusting herself to utter another word, Selena turned and left him.

Intending to be awake and away from the penthouse early enough to avoid seeing him, she was furious with herself, next morning, for sleeping in. Pearl woke her, an unheard-of precedent, as it was unusual for her to surface before midday when she wasn't working.

'Sorry,' Selena gasped, scrambling around for her wrap, when at last she began to believe Pearl really was sitting on the end of her bed, 'I didn't mean to over-sleep.'

'I'm not surprised you did,' Pearl snapped, 'seeing whom you were out with last night! I imagine you've exhausted yourself with wildly impossible dreams?'

'Out with . . .?' Selena croaked.

'Darling, you should know better than to try and pretend with me,' Pearl was still snapping in a drawling kind of way. 'I've just had Max Heger himself on the phone, telling me all about it.'

'All . . .?' Colour flooded Selena's cheeks hotly and Pearl's eyes sharpened.

'Just what's going on, Selena?'

'Why, nothing's going on!' Selena drew the edges her silky robe together tightly. Nothing, her morning nerves screamed, but a lot of soul-shaking kisses which no one must know about. Her senses disorganised again, even to remember them briefly, she hastened, 'Mr Heger merely asked me out for a drink, then we danced. He didn't seem prepared to listen when I said I'd like to get home around midnight, and I didn't like to insist. I was frightened, if I did, that it might spoil your chances of getting the part you want in his next film.'

Pearl paused, her mood changing slightly. 'I do want this part,' she admitted warily, 'but not if you're to be sacrificed.'

'Sacrificed?'

'Oh, for goodness' sake!' Pearl exclaimed. 'Stop squeaking like a two-year-old. You must understand what I'm talking about!'

Squashing down a cold hint of suspicion, Selena replied resolutely. 'If you're suggesting that Mr Heger mightn't give you the part unless I have an affair with him then I'm sure you're wrong.'

'Really?' Pearl was openly contemptuous of Selena's confidence. 'He's no schoolboy, to be as obvious as that. I doubt if he'll ask you to have an affair with him or anything else. He'll just sit back and wait for it all to happen.'

'Based on his past performances, I suppose?' Selena kept her voice cool with an effort, angry herself, now, that Pearl should believe her such an innocent.

'No one ever sees anything that man does unless he wishes it,' Pearl almost hissed, 'but one thing few people can ever stop is rumour. And believe me, my child, there's always plenty of that around Max Heger.'

'It won't be about me, so you can stop worrying,' Selena retorted shortly. 'He's not my type, besides being too old for me.'

'Thirty-four, maybe five,' Pearl's pencilled eyebrows rose. 'Come off it, darling! You aren't exactly a child, if you sometimes act like one, and even when Max is sixty he'll still have more than enough vitality to keep up with anyone of your age.'

Although Selena could well believe it, she refused to admit it. 'It's unlikely I'll know him then,' she said distantly.

'Then isn't important—now is,' Pearl replied tersely. 'If he took you out last night merely on impulse, to fill a boring hour, why does he want to see you again this morning?'

'This morning?' Try as she might, Selena couldn't hide her consternation. 'What's he been saying to you? He can't seriously want to see me again?'

'Idiot!' Pearl fumed, jumping up and tearing her hair with long scarlet talons. 'Hasn't he just been on about it! And he isn't a man to be making idle remarks on the telephone at eight in the morning. Selena must be there, he said, and he means it!'

'Well, I won't be there—I mean here,' Selena stammered uneasily, with an unusual disregard for Pearl's temper.

Looking more inflamed by the minute, Pearl snapped, 'You'd better be, honey.' Her eyes went over Selena's bewildered young face impatiently. 'I might be as puzzled as you, but unless you're here I have a feeling I can kiss goodbye to any hope of getting in on Max's next production. And,' she added with icy deliberation, 'if you don't stay and I don't get a part, you can certainly say goodbye to me!'

For a tense moment the two girls stared at each other, but as usual, Selena was the one who gave in. 'You win,' she said reluctantly. 'After all, where else could I go, and you never had to have me, in the first place.'

'Now we don't need to go into that!' Pearl said hastily. 'And don't be so bitter. Your parents may have neglected you a bit, but I don't suppose they're any worse than thousands of others. You should have learnt to accept this long ago.'

Immediately remorseful, Selena apologised. 'I hope you don't think I'm ungrateful, Pearl, but I still believe they should have looked after me themselves, instead of palming me off on to you.'

'I haven't complained,' Pearl shrugged, 'and I haven't asked much of you until now.'

'I know,' Selena said humbly, 'and I'm grateful, you know that, but you can't hold me wholly responsible for Mr Heger's decisions. As soon as I'm able, though, I'm going to find a place of my own.'

'Sure, sure,' Pearl agreed hurriedly, her ill temper fading as quickly as it had arisen, 'but I don't really mind having you, honey. In fact, at times you're very useful. If I was annoyed with you just now, it's simply because I'm very anxious to get this business with Max settled before I go off on holiday.'

'Yes, I suppose so,' Selena sighed, feeling trapped. 'I promise if I can help I will, but I'm serious about finding my own place.'

'Of course, and I would never try to keep you against your will.' All benevolence, once she had her own way Pearl smiled, her charm as warm as her beauty. More anxiously she glanced at the time. 'Now I think we'd both better get a move on or Max will be here before we're ready for him.'

'I'll hurry,' Selena nodded reluctantly.

Obviously relieved by Selena's continuing willingness to co-operate, Pearl paused on her way out. 'I tell you what,' she suggested, over her shoulder at the younger girl. 'If you're really serious about having your own pad, when I return from Bermuda I could perhaps find a buyer for that old place you've been left in Devon. It's sure to be worth something.'

While she showered, Selena thought with renewed interest about the house she had been bequeathed. She hadn't seen it as she hadn't yet been able to afford the train fare; it took almost everything she earned to pay Pearl for her board and lodgings. It had been left to her by another distant relative—she hadn't the faintest idea why, but she had been told by the solicitor dealing with the will that it was in an extremely bad condition. However, as Pearl sensibly pointed out, it must be worth something, and even a small amount might be enough to set her up in a small flat of her own.

A half an hour later Max Heger arrived, and by this time Selena's nerves were so taut she knew if she didn't manage to control them she might easily find herself running back to her room and locking the door.

For all she had promised Pearl she would do her best to help, she was aware of mixed feelings. Her first meeting with Max Heger had been an experience which had shaken her, but one she had hoped to forget. To meet him again, after she had ruled out such a possibility, had shattered her more than she cared to admit. Yet not even her most apprehensive moment had prepared her for the way she had felt when he had kissed her for the second time. With very little persuasion she might have let him do as he liked with her, as they had lain together so closely on the settee in his lounge. To her shame, she felt she would remember it for ever and, in demanding to see her this morning, she wondered if he intended making sure she did. Unhappily confused, she dusted sweetly scented talcum powder on her still damp body, trying not to recall how he had crushed her to him, the almost savage pressure of his arms and limbs.

Pearl was wearing the kind of daring, offbeat dress that reflected her flamboyant personality and made Selena in her sedate jeans and shirt feel positively plain. As if seeking to add to the sense of obscurity such an outfit gave her, she had tied her thick hair back with a tight ribbon, little dreaming that such tactics only served to emphasise the singular beauty of her other features. On impulse, taking no notice of Pearl's impatient sigh, she huddled in a somewhat ungainly heap in a deep armchair, contrarily determined to give the worst impression possible.

When the doorbell rang Pearl went to answer it herself, while Selena stayed where she was, feeling curiously rigid.

'Hello, Max!' Selena heard Pearl's voice rounded with pleasure. Pearl was adept at sounding warm and welcoming whenever a man appeared, and in the theatrical circles she moved in everyone was on first-name terms.

There was the usual formal reply from Max Heger, even a brief comment about the nip in the air, then they were in the lounge beside her.

'Hello, Selena.' Tall, his shoulders broad under a well fitting jacket, Max came straight towards her, holding out a hand she felt obliged to take. As he caught it in his larger one she flinched from the immediate sparks of contact, drawing quickly back, scarcely noticing the large package he was carrying under his arm. It wasn't until she saw Pearl's glance fixed on the famous label that she wondered about it briefly.

'Good morning, Mr Heger,' she replied primly, pulling free her fingers, which he seemed reluctant to part with, her small face with her large, slightly tilted eyes unconsciously guarded.

'Max,' he corrected, but automatically, as if he was thinking of something else. To her surprise he lifted the parcel he carried, dropping it into her lap. 'For you,' he smiled. 'A small present for agreeing to come out with me last night, and for any inconvenience I might have caused you.'

Whatever could he be thinking about? Whatever could it be? Selena stared at the bulky package in complete confusion. 'I—whether you inconvenienced me or not, Mr Heger, I don't accept presents from men, particularly ones I don't know.'

Pearl's eyes were almost popping. 'Aren't you going to open it, though?' She was full of curiosity and obviously didn't understand Selena's reluctance. In fact, while Selena hesitated and Max Heger stood enigmatically by, she undertook to open it herself.

Both girls gasped as a beautiful fur jacket was revealed. 'Mink!' Pearl breathed, her eyes wide with surprise and envy.

'Selena said she'd been forced to borrow your coat last night, as she hadn't one of her own,' Max Heger said suavely.

'Well, she was certainly in the right company when she complained,' Pearl laughed sharply, her voice and laughter so insinuating no one could have misunderstood what she was thinking, least of all Selena, who felt at any moment she was in danger of exploding with fury.

CHAPTER THREE

'YOU'RE a very lucky girl,' said Pearl, adding tartly, 'And much cleverer than I realised.'

'Perhaps,' Selena replied, tight-lipped, 'but I don't happen to want a gift like this, nor will I accept it. I'd have been more pleased with a bag of sweets.'

Her blue eyes widened on the beautiful gleaming fur which Pearl still held almost reverently. Quickly she snatched it from her, thrusting it back into Max Heger's arms. 'There you are, Mr Heger,' she exclaimed. 'Go and try it on someone else!'

'You refuse to have it?' he frowned, his face visibly darkening.

'I've just said so, haven't I?' Her lips curled as her eyes met his coldly. 'Don't you understand plain English?'

'I understand plain insolence,' he snarled suddenly, red rage seeping under his hard jawbone.

'Just as long as you get the message,' she flung back furiously, discretion forgotten.

'I certainly do,' he returned, his voice and eyes freezing. 'I can take a hint as good as the next man. You've managed to convey it quite charmingly. You don't want anything more to do with me, or from me. I'd simply be wasting my time if I offered anything else. Now I'll be going.'

'Hi, wait a minute!' Pearl cried, as if only just realising what he was saying. 'None of this is my fault, Max. I've done nothing to set Selena against you, but I thought you were coming to see me?'

On his way to the door, he paused, but so grimly that Selena quailed. He looked as black as the devil and about as tolerant. He was like a man who, on finding

his chosen course strewn with obstacles, was consumed
by an alien, violent desire to kick them out of his way.
'Yes, I did,' he confirmed, turning back again.

'Then I don't understand . . .' Pearl began.

'Think of it this way,' Max cut in with sarcastic coolness. 'If your cousin won't accept one thing, she's as
likely to refuse another. And,' he added curtly, 'if she
dislikes me so much she can't be civil, how could we
ever work together?'

'But I'm talking about a film contract, which only
involves me!' Pearl wailed, casting Selena a venomous
look. 'I don't know what's going on, but please, Max,
don't make me suffer for something I know nothing
about!'

'I shouldn't dream of it,' he said smoothly, but still
with a flinty glint in his eye. 'I have to tell you, though,
that your prospects do rely to a certain extent on
Selena, and she doesn't seem interested.'

'Just what are you getting at, Mr Heger?' Selena
gasped, before Pearl could intervene. She didn't really
want to know, but she didn't care to see Pearl kept in
such tormenting suspense. And if Pearl's uncertain
temper blew, it could mean the end of any chance she
had of getting anything from Max Heger. Gulping
hastily, she looked at him, her voice falling to a half
pleading whisper. 'Couldn't you please explain?'

Gratified by her more humble demeanour, he met her
eyes silkily. 'If you're willing to listen.'

For Pearl's sake she felt she could do nothing else.
Unhappily she nodded.

Taking her utterly by surprise, Max said suavely, 'I'll
be brief. For the part Pearl hopes to get in my new film,
which is set in the last century, she has to have a maid.
It's a small part but necessary, and I want you to have
it, Selena.'

'Me?'

'Why not? I believe you've had small parts before?'

Selena gazed at him speechless and saw the obstinate

set of his chin. 'Once, when I was twelve, I had a very small part in rep with my father. He insisted, but I hated it and was glad to get back to school. I've done nothing since.'

'That's of no consequence,' he swept her protests aside as though he had scarcely listened to them. 'You won't be asked to do anything difficult, and I'll give you all the help you need.'

His kindness, if that was what it really was, only alarmed Selena more, although she couldn't have said exactly why. 'No, Mr Heger. I'm sorry, I couldn't.' Her refusal was involuntary, but even so, she tried to be gracious, and her face paled before his renewed displeasure.

Pearl interrupted sharply, as bewildered as Selena, but obviously of the opinion that Selena was quite out of her mind not to jump at such a chance—a chance, she was sure, any other girl would mortgage her soul for. 'I don't see why you shouldn't do it, Selena. I think it's a very good idea, and I'm used to having you around.'

Which was another way of conveying how much Pearl considered she owed her. This Selena realised and admitted, but she still shook her head. 'No, I'm sorry.'

Again, before Max Heger could erupt, Pearl forestalled him quickly. 'Let me talk to her, Max. I'm sure I'll be able to persuade her. She's only doing some typing for a writer, which shouldn't be difficult to give up.'

'A man?' Max Heger's voice couldn't have been colder.

'Yes.' Selena flushed as she recalled giving Max the impression she wasn't working. 'And he's nice,' she stared at Max defiantly, 'I couldn't let him down.'

'Who is he?' Max went white with rage.

'Don't ask me,' Pearl shrugged, when Selena didn't reply and Max glanced at her. 'He's a professor or something like that, I believe.'

Infuriated, Selena exclaimed, 'His name happens to be Ronald Walker, he's quite famous in his own field, and I owe him a lot.' Which wasn't strictly true, as she worked for everything she got. However, if it helped her to fight Max Heger, wasn't anything worth trying?

Max Heger's mouth tightened savagely. 'What about Pearl, here? Hasn't she been good to you?'

'I try my best,' Pearl murmured, acting the part of an angel with flair. 'In return I've never asked much.'

'Until now,' Max sympathised softly, staring frostily at Selena over Pearl's pathetically bent head.

Stubbornly Selena stared back, not bothering to hide her own anger. She resented the way he treated her. The way he seemed to consider there was nothing out of the ordinary in the pressures he had put on her since they had met. This morning's effort must be his best, it had her still reeling with shock, but what she resented most was that he had involved Pearl. He was going to make Pearl hate her, and Pearl's hatred was no pleasant thing! Selena had witnessed examples of it before. She had heard her ranting and rating against people who had supposedly offended her. She had seen her spiteful, hurtful revenge. During the next two weeks, before she left for Bermuda, if Pearl didn't get her own way she might easily make Selena's life a living hell.

'You know I'm grateful for what you've done for me,' she dragged her eyes back to Pearl, repeating what she had said many times. 'Please don't let us fall out over this. I'd really be hopeless as your maid.'

'Of course you wouldn't,' Max Heger snapped, cutting in. 'It entails very little, otherwise I shouldn't have suggested it. The part Pearl would like, though, is important. She plays a beautiful but two-timing lady, intent on marrying a wealthy man in order to procure his vast estates for her lover. You, Selena, give the game away and win the lifelong gratitude of our hero and his true lady.'

'It sounds a bit too naïve for me,' Selena said scornfully. 'Is there any particular reason why I should be this paragon of a maid? I'm sure you must know dozens of other girls who'd be only too willing to oblige?'

'I know of several.' Surprisingly, Pearl came to her aid, and Selena smiled at her gratefully before turning hopefully to Max Heger.

'No,' to her dismay he was obdurate, 'I've made up my mind. Time is going to be more than usually important in my next production, Pearl, which means everything must run smoothly, and while I'll admit you're ideal for this part you can be temperamental.'

'I'm not the only one,' Pearl protested indignantly.

He agreed, but with reservations. 'Forgive me, my dear,' he added blandly, 'but the time for plain speaking is rarely after the shooting begins. You can be worse than most. The last time I worked with you, I remember, everything was disrupted for days when you took an inexplicable dislike to one of the cast.'

'That wasn't my fault!'

'It never is,' he replied dryly. 'But it occurred to me that as you live with Selena it would almost be a case of carrying on much as you're doing now. I don't often have such brilliant flashes of inspiration,' he finished softly, while managing to convey what seemed to Selena something very like a subtle threat.

Cold with dislike, she stared at him. He was plausible. He sounded convincing. If she hadn't felt instinctively that, on this occasion, he was far from sincere, she might have believed him. Normally, she believed, he wouldn't give a young, untrained girl a second thought, let alone a part in his new film.

'You mean you won't consider Pearl if I don't agree?' she asked incredulously.

'No,' he said firmly, glancing at Pearl again. 'If you're prepared to wait, Pearl, to see if she changes her mind, then it's up to you.'

'Oh, I'm sure Selena will,' Pearl smiled, the glint in her eye daring Selena not to.

'I won't.' Ignoring the glint, Selena swallowed with determination. Even if she had craved to be an actress,

which she did not, she would never risk spending perhaps several months with Max Heger. She had an unhappy suspicion that were she to do so she might never
be the same again.

Pearl, obviously in danger of losing her temper
completely, paused. As if Max Heger wasn't the only
one to have flashes of inspiration she exclaimed archly,
'You won't know, Selena, that a lot of this film is to be
shot in Devon, so if you do as Max asks you might be
able to persuade him to buy the old house you've been
left. You do need one on the moors for some of the
scenes, don't you?' she appealed to him.

His eyes narrowed slightly with a quick glint. 'A lot
of things might be possible, if Selena decides to be sensible,' he returned enigmatically. 'But I think she should
have time to think it over.' Before Selena could deny
this, he silenced her with a piercing glance. 'I have to go
now, but I'd like you and Pearl to join me this evening.'
As she drowned despairingly in his cool grey eyes, he
named a famous West End hotel. '

Feeling more trapped than ever, Selena watched
silently as Pearl hastened to follow him to the door. She
heard Pearl assuring him that they would both be there,
but in his arrogance, she realised, he hadn't waited for
an answer. He had simply taken it for granted that they
would be humbly delighted to comply.

When Pearl came back from ushering the great man
out, she launched straight into the attack. 'You can't
really be serious about turning Max's offer down—as
well as his fabulous fur coat?'

Feeling years older of a sudden, Selena retorted
sharply, 'You of all people shouldn't need to be told
that one's as ridiculous as the other!'

'Maybe,' Pearl shrugged. 'But directors sometimes
enjoy being ridiculous. He's not the first I've known to
suffer from some mild form of insanity, and in his position he can get away with it. Other people have moods,
which Max doesn't allow,' she shrugged bitterly, 'but

heaven help anyone who gets in the way of his little whims!'

'Well, I don't intend being one of them,' Selena snapped, irritated that she felt so shaken.

Pearl snapped right back, 'You could do worse—a lot worse! I find it difficult to believe he fancies you, personally. The women he usually escorts obviously know what they're doing, but you'd be a fool not to take what you can get. He's rumoured to be about the wealthiest man in the business, and a pretty high-powered one at that. There's also a rumour going that he's about to retire from producing, so this could be a once-in-a-lifetime chance.'

'No . . .' Selena began hotly, then hesitated more cautiously. Why risk quarrelling, perhaps irrevocably, with Pearl if it wasn't necessary? Quite likely, before the day was out Max Heger might have changed his mind. 'Please, Pearl,' she entreated, 'let's wait until we see him again. I think you'll find he'll have had second thoughts about me—when he's had time to cool down. You know what men are like.'

This appealed to Pearl's sense of humour. A little of her angry impatience disappeared and she contented herself with a cynical laugh. 'I do, honey, but I don't think you've a clue. You're a babe in arms when it comes to cool types like Max. If he liked, I suspect he could reduce you to nothing, in more ways than one, so you'd better think twice before saying no to him again.'

Trying not to feel caught between her dependency on Pearl and the dangerous determination she sensed in Max Heger, Selena dressed quickly, and without much concentration for dinner with him that evening. She had just tied the sash on her best beige cotton when Pearl burst into her bedroom with an exclamation of dismay.

'Heaven help us, that will never do! Take it off at once!' she commanded imperiously.

'I've nothing else,' Selena replied. If she felt sorry for herself it wasn't because of her inadequate wardrobe.

'No one's going to notice me!'

'The only one who matters might.' Pearl was weighing Selena up sharply, as if she had never properly seen her before. 'You're thinner than I am, but I'm sure I can find something to fit you. Take that dishrag you're wearing off and come with me!'

An hour later, when they arrived at the hotel, Selena felt she was another person. The dress she wore now was almost new and surprisingly demure, apart from the neckline, which was low enough to expose quite a lot of Selena's slim young figure. When she had protested, Pearl had merely waved her doubts aside and told her not to be so silly. It was high time Selena grew up a bit, she said. She had gone on to do simple but expert things to Selena's hair and face, cleverly drawing her attention to something else. She had shown her how to make the most of her looks and had been so generous with her help and advice that Selena had felt it would be churlish to protest any further.

Max Heger met them himself, drawing them quickly towards the rather dazzling group of people he was talking to. Casually he took Selena's arm as he introduced her, but there was nothing casual about the close glance he swept over her when, formalities complete, they were for a brief moment alone.

He didn't speak, and she had the strange feeling of being on an island, just the two of them, isolated from the world. She felt her senses reaching out to him and suddenly found her heart beating fast with excitement. Swiftly she lowered her thick lashes to hide her eyes for fear they should betray her treacherous emotions.

As he sighed and moved away, still without speaking, it took quite a bit of willpower not to watch him go. Yet even with her eyes lowered over the glass of sherry he had given her, she could still see him. Impressed on her mind was his lean, handsome face, his height and width of shoulder, the distinctive set of his dark head.

Though he didn't pay her a great deal of attention

beforehand, he had her sitting beside him during dinner. 'Well, are you glad you decided to come?' he asked dryly, as the woman on his other side spoke to someone else.

Mutinously her eyes met his. 'You didn't give me much choice.'

'I'm starting the way I mean to go on,' he warned deviously. 'You're looking beautiful.' His eyes swept her closely again, but this time were far more intimate in their appraisal. Selena felt them lingering on her shadowed cleavage, the seductive curves of her breasts.

Was his manner faintly taunting? Fiercely she wanted to tell him the dress hadn't been her idea, but for some unknown reason Pearl had begged her not to. It was becoming painfully clear, however, that Max Heger laboured under the impression that girls who wore clothes like this were begging for all they got.

'You've told me I'm beautiful before,' she said angrily, her cheeks pink, her eyes defiant.

'Your way of receiving a compliment, I suppose?' One dark brow rose. 'Why don't you react like other women?'

'You mean, to you, Mr Heger?' she challenged sharply, striving to keep her wits beneath the intimate depth of his surveillance. 'Are you used to having them swooning at your feet?'

'One day you might,' he threatened, his jaw tightening.

'I don't think so.' Drawing a deep breath, Selena stared down at the delicious entrée before her, wondering how on earth she was going to manage it with shaking fingers. Everything here was the height of opulence. Not often might she have the chance of dining in a place like this, and she wished he would leave her alone to enjoy it instead of making her tremble with the narrowed insolence in his eyes and the things he was saying.

'Don't be too sure,' he said curtly, as though her contrariness continued to annoy him. 'Possibly before this evening is out you'll find you no longer want to keep on fighting me.'

Again she wondered what he was hinting at. Surely he didn't mean to start pestering her about joining the cast of his new film here? 'It must be very nice to be so full of confidence,' she retorted coldly.

With an abruptness that startled her, he asked, 'Why wouldn't you accept the present I bought you?'

'I hope the store was agreeable to taking it back?' she countered sweetly.

'Which doesn't answer my question.'

Indignantly she glared at him, not caring who might notice, unable to believe he couldn't work it out for himself. 'Do you really want to know, Mr Heger?'

His sensuous mouth curled in a sneer which must have been as obvious as Selena's hostility. 'I shouldn't set myself up as a paragon of virtue, or even try to, if I were you. Not while you're still living with someone like Miss Burnett.'

Selena almost choked. 'It's a wonder you ever condescended to invite us here? Weren't you afraid we might contaminate your fine friends? Let me see—didn't I count three titles?'

'You did,' he acknowledged tightly, 'but that has nothing at all to do with it. Most of them might be admired for their lack of pretence, if nothing else, and the majority manage to hold down a job while living decent, hard-working lives.'

'And I don't give this impression?'

'Not in a dress like the one you're wearing at the moment and downing whiskys as you were doing last night!' Tauntingly he smiled. 'No use trying to annihilate me with those beautiful blue eyes. You'd have to be more convincing than that before I'd believe you.'

'I won't even try,' she averted her glance. 'You're even worse than I thought.'

'Attack your dinner, not me,' he snapped indifferently.

For the rest of the meal, which seemed to go on for

an unconscionable time, Selena saw little more than the taut angle of his jaw in profile. Because of this she was grateful for the attention of her other neighbour, a young man called Alan White, who appeared flatteringly delighted to talk to her. Before coffee was served they had exchanged names and telephone numbers, her new friend even attempting to make a date with her for the following evening. It was an invitation she was reluctantly forced to refuse, however, as she dared not ask Ronald Walker for three evenings off in the same week.

It wasn't until around midnight that she realised suddenly that Pearl was nowhere to be seen. When, after several more minutes, she still couldn't spot her, Selena was driven to approach Max Heger. He was deep in conversation with a glamorous blonde, but turned to her willingly enough. 'Do you know where Pearl is?' she asked anxiously.

'I've no idea,' he confessed sardonically, his eyes glinting on Selena's pale young face. 'I did promise her I'd take you home, but I never thought to ask where she was off to. She was with Lew Adams, though,' lightly he named another of his guests, a well-known actor, 'I expect she'll be safe enough.'

Hating his sarcasm, Selena exclaimed. 'That's all I need to know. I can get myself home, thank you. Or,' she couldn't resist smiling, with false smugness, 'perhaps Alan would take me?'

'No, he won't,' Max rejected the idea curtly, clamping steely fingers around her thin wrist. 'Remember Pearl's future could be at stake,' he threatened softly. 'Fight me too hard and you'll soon discover exactly what that means.'

Half desperately, Selena gazed back at him, not sure what to do for the best. In spite of his derisive opinion of Pearl, she knew she wasn't all that bad. Come to that—bitterly she considered Max Heger's darkly handsome features—who was he to criticise? His private life might stand an even less closer scrutiny than Pearl's.

Yet there was no denying he was a force to be reckoned with in the film industry. He could probably make or break an actress with one snap of the long decisive fingers which seemed at the moment in danger of breaking her arm.

It was incredible and not really possible, Selena silently argued, that he should be seriously interested in someone like herself. It was merely a whim, she assured herself, as she had done before. A sudden interest which might as quickly subside. After which he might be more than willing to give Pearl the part she desired, and to dismiss Selena North from his thoughts as a girl who had wasted too much of his time. If only, Selena thought despairingly, her senses could be controlled as sensibly. It was completely illogical that they should react so crazily whenever Max came near her.

Half an hour later, as she sat in a taxi beside him, after the dinner party had dispersed, she realised he was under the impression that he had only to threaten a little and she would obey. Even so, now he had the opportunity, he didn't once mention the part he wanted her to take in his new film, and she was convinced more than ever that he was simply using this as a means of getting his own way over something else.

To her dismay he didn't ask the taxi to wait. 'Why don't you go straight on?' she suggested hopefully. 'I'll be quite all right now.'

He slipped the driver a note and waved him on. 'I was hoping you would ask me in for a drink,' he drawled.

'Not a repetition of last night?' Selena said sharply, stung by something in his manner to refer to it again.

Mockingly reproving, he replied. 'You think all I want to do is kiss you?'

Colour flared under her skin as he took the key from her fumbling fingers and opened the penthouse door. 'I'm sorry,' she tried to speak evenly. 'Perhaps I'm wrong. But as we scarcely know each other, what can we have to talk about?'

'If we're to get to know each other, we have to begin somewhere,' he pointed out reasonably, 'and if you don't believe in short cuts talking seems the only other way.'

She had a peculiar feeling he was laughing at her. Hating it, she retorted, 'You must be kept busy if you're willing to go to such lengths with every girl you meet!' In the lounge she let Pearl's old fur jacket slip from her slender shoulders to the huge modern settee, ignoring his frown.

'Not every girl,' he shrugged. 'Some don't encourage a man to waste time. They're usually only too willing to agree to whatever I have in mind. And a lot more,' he added cynically, 'which is only in their minds. Now,' he asked coolly, 'how about my drink?'

'I don't believe you really want one, Mr Heger.' She moved back a pace with a cool flare of defiance.

'Mr Heger!' he jeered suddenly. 'If there's one thing guaranteed to infuriate me, it's your stubborn refusal to call me Max.' Before she could guess his intentions, his hands went out to haul her to him. 'Say it,' he commanded. 'Say my name, Selena.'

'No.' Irrationally, if she did, she feared it would remove her only defence against him. The formal Mr mightn't be much, but it was better than nothing. 'I'd rather not,' she entreated him silently, begging him not to insist.

He ignored the appeal in her dazzling blue eyes. There was about him an intentness, a hint of excitement held firmly in check. 'Perhaps I must persuade you to change your mind,' he said softly.

As he bent his dark head towards her she felt a sudden rush of panic and lifted her hands blindly to push him away. As he pulled her ruthlessly closer, her efforts were humiliatingly reduced. She might well have tried to thrust aside a mountain for all the success she had. He was all bone and muscle and hard determination, and with her lesser strength she could never hope to fight him effectively.

He kissed her slowly, almost lazily, but when she persisted in struggling the pressure of his mouth deepened in a slightly brutal insolence. Again her whole body began dissolving into liquid fire, the pulse in her throat racing madly. Max kissed her insistently until her lips parted helplessly and she grew terrified of the response he was so expertly arousing. Her mind reeled. It was as if she was standing outside herself, watching herself drown in a sensuous flood of desire.

Wildly she wanted to press herself close to him, to savour more intimately the sensations sweeping her, feel his hands caressing her. His mouth, warm and sensually demanding, moved over hers, crushing its softness, while his fingers threaded her silky hair, holding her still. Faintly she whimpered, a wild tremor running through her as she instinctively arched her slender limbs against his.

Then she was free. Just as suddenly as he had taken hold of her, Max thrust her away, leaving her to wonder dazedly why she had been released so quickly. A moment ago, for all her senses had been reeling, she could have sworn he had meant to go on amusing himself for quite a while longer.

He went to study briefly a painting, a surrealistic effort by a famous French artist, long since dead. It had been left to Pearl by a wealthy aunt and she was inordinately proud of it, but Selena doubted, somehow, that Max Heger would care for it at all.

He turned, his expressive brows lifting wryly. 'After I said I wouldn't . . . Why do you provoke me?'

'I'm sorry, Max.' She hadn't the immediate strength to deny she had.

A faint smile curved the mouth which only minutes ago had dealt so thoroughly with hers. 'Well, at least it achieved something.'

Blankly she watched a flicker of dry amusement lighten

the smouldering darkness of his eyes. 'Oh, I see.'

Again he smiled. 'Perhaps we've both achieved something? I've actually managed to make you speak my name, and in turn you've got rid of me.'

'Rid of you?'

He met the bewildered enquiry in her eyes blandly. 'Isn't that what you've been trying to do ever since I brought you home?'

He exclaimed, when she flushed. 'Don't bother to deny it. I do intend going, but before I do, I just want to say that I haven't changed my mind about having you in my next film.'

Selena's heart sank. So much for the hopes she had been entertaining! 'You still want me as Pearl's maid?' she asked dully.

'Yes.' He didn't elaborate or say more, he merely stared at her grimly then swung around and left her. At the door he paused, 'I don't know if it would have helped you to reach a decision if I'd taken you to bed a few minutes ago. I could have obliged quite easily, but I'd prefer, when I do, to be safe from possible interruptions.'

For almost a week Selena saw nothing more of Max and, after the shock of his final withering remarks, she was glad. Weakly she began hoping he had forgotten her, in spite of his threats. She tried hard to forget him, but whenever her thoughts turned to him she was consumed by such a mixture of longing and dislike that it left her trembling and apprehensive.

Then Pearl dropped a terrible bombshell, one that Selena felt she could well have done without. Late on Friday evening, as Selena returned from typing her professor's manuscripts, she informed her that they were to spend the weekend with Max.

'He rang, only an hour ago,' she announced smugly, 'and asked us both down to Lynton for a couple of nights. Naturally I accepted.'

'But I can't go!' Selena exclaimed, suddenly happy she didn't have to invent an excuse. 'Don't you remember, I told you before I went out, I promised Ronald I'd work the whole day tomorrow.'

'Oh, that's no problem,' Pearl laughed. 'I've just been in touch with the professor and told him you won't be there. I thought it would save time.'

Dazed, Selena gazed at her. 'You—you rang Ronald? What did he say?'

Pearl shrugged indifferently. 'He was upset, but not nearly so much as he might have been if I'd mentioned it to Max and left him to deal with it.'

'He wouldn't have dared!' Selena gasped.

'Darling, you don't know Max Heger.'

'Nor do I want to,' Selena retorted fiercely. 'I'm certainly not going to—wherever was it you said?'

Feeling near to tears at such effrontery, Selena blinked. Damn Max Heger! Why couldn't he leave them alone?

'Lynton—a super place in Berkshire. I've talked to people who've been there. You'll love it, Selena.'

'I don't even want to see it!'

'You'll have to go, honey.' Pearl's patience was swiftly evaporating, as she recognised that Selena was far from willing. 'In heaven's name!' she cried. 'How many people do you think he asks there even for a meal, never mind a weekend? We're honoured, sweetie, and you'd better believe it and forget about anything else.'

Didn't Pearl know she was asking the impossible? 'I can't see why we both have to go,' Selena said angrily. 'Why can't you go by yourself?'

'Gladly I would,' Pearl snapped, 'but he wants you. He appears determined on having you in his next production, and if you continue to be obstinate then we could both be out. And if that happens I'll never forgive you!'

'He might change his mind,' Selena suggested, on a note of quiet desperation.

'We can always hope so,' Pearl snapped again. 'But we've been through this all before, Selena.'

'He has a house in London.' Selena's stunned mind seemed to be on a seesaw, over which she was rapidly losing control.

'And another in Berkshire which his sister and her husband look after for him, as he isn't much there. It's common knowledge that he lives in America for most of the year. His mother was an American, I've heard, and this house was left to him by his English father.'

So he was half American, which explained the faint drawl. 'If I do agree to go, it will only be in the hope that he'll come to realise just how little potential I have as an actress,' Selena said at last, feeling cornered.

'Fair enough,' Pearl agreed grudgingly, 'but remember to make yourself pleasant, and to leave the prerogative of mind-changing to him. If not, there'll be hell to pay, so be warned!'

Next day, when Max arrived for them, he was driving his own car again and his mood seemed in keeping with the cool, frosty morning.

'Good morning, girls,' he flattered Pearl, who was at least ten years Selena's senior. He bestowed on Pearl a lazy grin which faded quickly as he turned to Selena. 'Missed me?' he asked, as Pearl moved in front of them out of the lift.

'Of course,' she replied, wanting to shout no, but mindful of Pearl's threats.

'How much?' He looked at her keenly, as if quite aware of rubbing salt into a wound.

'You'll never know,' she replied with acid sweetness.

'I'd like to.' Sardonically he caught her arm, pulling her to a stop as Pearl walked on.

If it hadn't been for Pearl, she didn't know what she might have said. Uneasily she stirred beneath the hand that held her. While she didn't owe Pearl all that much, considering the chores she did, where had she to go, if Pearl threw her out? 'I'm sorry, Max,' with a great effort she managed to look serene, 'I had noticed you haven't been around.'

'You surprise me.' His eyes narrowed.

'I was surprised myself by your invitation. It was so unexpected.' Rather shakily she tried to avert her eyes from his ruthless face, unwilling to admit that, with his dark good looks and powerful figure, he was a superb example of manhood.

'Don't you like the unexpected?' he queried suavely. 'I hope it didn't put you out?'

'No—at least . . .' With a dismayed exclamation she broke off. She must give Ronald a ring. In the hectic scramble to pack her own clothes and then Pearl's, it had gone right out of her head. As Max turned her towards the car again, she hung back. 'There is something. I have to make a phone call—I've just remembered.' Beseechingly she gazed up at him. 'If you go to the car and wait for me, I shan't be many minutes.'

CHAPTER FOUR

IT was only good manners to give Ronald a ring. Pearl might not have explained properly. She very rarely did if it wasn't to further her own ends, and she could be abrupt to the point of rudeness. Pearl wouldn't concern herself that Selena might not have a job to come back to. A horrible suspicion suddenly struck Selena that Pearl could have done her best to make sure Ronald found someone else to do his typing, thus leaving Selena with little alternative but to accept Max Heger's offer. All of which might happen if Selena didn't contact Ronald herself and make a personal apology.

Swiftly she ran from the lift to the apartment, nerves making her fingers so shaky she had to dial twice before she got through. Then he was ages in answering.

'Selena here, Ronald,' she said when he spoke. 'I'm sorry, I can't make it this morning.'

'So Miss Burnett informed me last night.' He sounded disturbed. He was put out, she could tell, that she wasn't going to be there.

'You don't realise how sorry I am.' She was speaking breathlessly but couldn't seem to help it. It must be agitation, and having to race along the corridor.

'You're sorry!' Over the line she could see his brow furrowing fretfully. 'Don't you understand, I can't do without you!'

'Nor can I do without you, Ronald!' Her voice rose. The few pounds a week he paid didn't amount to much, but it was all she had. 'I tell you what,' she went on recklessly, 'I'll come early on Monday and stay all night. I promise.'

'Can I believe that?' he grumbled, not noticeably appeased. 'I've never been able to persuade you to stay later than ten before.'

Selena forced a laugh, attempting a light joke in order to pacify him. 'Because I've never wanted to stay before, Ronald, but there has to be a first time, for every girl, I mean. Well, you know what I mean . . .' she faltered, feeling decidedly muddled.

'Won't Miss Burnett mind?'

'Not if I explain where I'll be. Pearl's always telling me I should grow up—so I intend to.'

'Well,' he mumbled thoughtfully, 'if we work all night we might just about manage it. You're sure?'

'Of course I'm sure. And I never go back on my word.'

'Goodbye, then.'

'Until Monday.'

Gently Selena replaced the receiver, an almost tender smile on her face as she pictured his absent-minded relief. Poor Ronald, he was always so unnecessarily harassed!

'Have you quite finished?'

Selena's nerves jumped again as she turned quickly to find Max in the doorway. She could see by the icy expression on his face that he was furious at being kept waiting. 'Sorry,' she stammered uneasily, her cheeks flushing too readily. 'It was a—a very personal call.'

The corner of his mouth curled and his eyes glinted as though he disliked her intensely. 'Of course,' he agreed curtly, 'but you could have chosen a better time.'

Bewildered, she frowned. She hadn't thought she'd been all that long, but Max wouldn't be tolerant of delays which weren't entirely of his own making. 'Well,' she hesitated, as he made no effort to move, 'we can go now.'

'If you're quite ready?' he rejoined sarcastically. Standing politely aside, he allowed her to pass before closing the door sharply behind them.

He sounded so icily disapproving that she found herself explaining involuntarily, 'I'm sorry, Max, but your invitation took me completely by surprise. I had made other arrangement, and I wanted to be sure someone understood.' She wasn't going to mention the professor by name and hear him sneered at!

Coolly he said. 'Do I take it that the thought of spending a weekend in the country home of a famous director drove everything else from your mind?'

'It could have been partly responsible,' she acknowledged cautiously, again thinking of Pearl.

As the lift stopped and they left it, Max glared at her. 'Only partly? Did it never occur to you that you could be getting too hard to please?'

'Girls who get around get choosey, Mr Heger,' she retorted, somewhat amazed at herself. While she had tried hard to equal his sophisticated sarcasm, she hadn't meant to come out with anything quite like that!

'You aren't telling me something I don't already know,' he rasped, and she felt the tenseness inside her grow as she caught the scorn in his swiftly hooded glance, as he thrust her less than gently into the back of a beautiful Mercedes.

Swallowing hard, she subsided on the soft leather seat, her breath momentarily leaving her. When Max was angry there was something about him that struck a primitive pulse deep inside her, leaving her shaken and weak. Bleakly she wondered why this man should have the power to affect her so. He was arrogant and overbearing, yet she must be the only one who wasn't impressed by him. His cool assumption of his own worth was not to be disputed. She grudgingly admitted that whatever other faults he had false pride was not one of them, or false humility.

Carefully she straightened the sleeve of her jacket which his savage hold on her arm had wrinkled. The suit she wore hadn't cost much, but it suited her. With its toning shirt and waistcoat it looked young and smartly fashionable. Surprisingly her father had sent her the money for it, a year ago, when she left school, and she had always thought she looked good in it. Yet Max Heger had scarcely spared her a second glance. He would be less than impressed with her, she realised, whatever she had on.

Her heart curiously heavy, she listened to him talking cordially to Pearl. Or was it Pearl who was talking to him? Selena wasn't sure. She was too busy trying to avoid studying the back of his head to take much notice of what was being said. When she became aware of him watching her in the driving mirror, she flushed deeply, as if he had caught her doing something wrong. Unhappily she looked away.

The only stop they made was for morning coffee, during which Selena again remained almost silent. Yet she didn't think either Max or Pearl noticed. They appeared to regard her pale face with indifference as they fell to discussing a film Max had made in this area several years ago about the Civil War. Max pointed out that Lynton, where they were going, was not that far from Donnington Castle, which had been successfully defended three times by the Royalist Sir John Boys. Selena concluded that this last information had been for her benefit as Pearl had been in the film and clearly remembered every detail. Selena regarded this as a better sign and was oddly grateful that Max must be feeling slightly friendlier towards her.

They reached Lynton, a lovely old manor house set in quiet Berkshire countryside, in time for lunch. A girl in her early thirties, whom Selena took to be Max's sister, came out to meet them.

'Oh, this is simply super!' she exclaimed extravagantly. 'I didn't expect to see you here again before you left for America, Max. I was quite surprised when your secretary rang to say you were coming.'

She was closely followed by three children and two dogs, and Max's explanation, if he made any, was lost in the general noise. 'Deirdre,' he said grimly, 'can't you control them?'

Pulling a wry face at him, Deirdre explained, 'Nurse is having her hair done in Newbury and I promised to look after them for an hour. You know how it is.'

'No, I do not,' he snapped. 'Where are the maids?'

'Oh, never mind.' Laughing, Deirdre turned to Pearl and Selena, whom Max briefly introduced. 'Please take no notice of my bad-tempered brother, he's not usually so grumpy.'

While Max heard her out with derisively raised brows, Selena was secretly amused to see how popular he was with the children, for all his disparaging remarks. They tangled themselves around his long legs, the youngest, a girl of no more than three or four, demanding to be picked up. When, with an audible sigh, Max obeyed, she clutched two chubby arms around his neck and kissed him.

'See what I mean?' Deirdre shrugged, as they turned, dogs and all, and went into the house.

'My husband will be here shortly,' she informed Pearl and Selena. 'Something's come up that he's had to sort out, but if you'd like to go upstairs before lunch he'll be back by the time you're down again.'

'We might have been wiser to have eaten before we arrived,' Max observed wryly, 'judging from the general state of things.'

'I've never known Max as short-tempered as he's been this trip,' Deirdre said frankly, as she showed them to their rooms. 'The children have their own wing and are never seen by visitors as a rule. They're completely shut off and he knows it. No, I think he has something on his mind.'

Rather startled by such outspokenness, which she was sure Max wouldn't appreciate, Selena made no reply. She heard Pearl suggesting that it could be his new film. 'He does have a lot on his mind.' She glanced at Selena vindictively.

'Possibly,' Deirdre nodded, not completely convinced. 'That's not for a while, though, and he's going back to the States next week. He might find a solution to what's bothering him there. I hope so. Kit, that's my husband, and I are going with him, so are the children. We're looking forward to it enormously, but it won't be the same if Max is in a bad mood.'

Selena was glad when, after taking her to another room further along the corridor, Deirdre left her. Deirdre's frankness was appealing, but it was also a bit overwhelming. Selena, with her collection of parents and step-parents, had grown so used to having to think cautiously before saying anything that such natural exuberance was now strange to her.

A sharp knock on her door, almost before she had closed it, startled her. Thinking that Deirdre had forgotten something, she called for her to come in, but it was Max who opened the door and stepped inside.

Her eyes wide, Selena stared at him enquiringly. In some inexplicable way, his coming here like this had seemed to change their relationship entirely. Her heart began hammering so loudly she couldn't speak.

'Have you everything you want?' he asked at last. 'Before we left the hotel where we had coffee I rang and told Deirdre to have this room ready for you. It's next to my own and I thought you might enjoy the view.'

'Why, yes,' she stammered, unable to help herself. 'I—I haven't had time to look out the window yet, but the room is lovely, thank you.' She was surprised and grateful that he had gone to so much trouble on her account. 'I'm just going to wash before lunch,' she added awkwardly.

His eyes never left her face, and while his regard was intent there was no particular kindness in it. 'I'll send a maid to unpack for you.'

'Oh, no, I can manage myself. Really I can.' She flushed when she thought of the few cheap clothes she had brought with her. Maids in houses like this could be much more snobbish than those they waited on. She knew, because some of her school friends lived in big houses and occasionally she had stayed with them.

Ignoring her protests, Max took a quick step towards her, then stopping abruptly he thrust his hands in his trouser pockets. He had removed his jacket, she saw. Presumably he had been to his own room, and his chest muscles expanded when he drew a deep breath. Again she had the impression that he was fighting with cold anger and impatience and it made her unhappy. Bleakly she wished she had been the kind of girl willing to do anything a man asked, or that, in turn, Max didn't ask the impossible.

Eventually he spoke, after they had stared at each other for several tense moments. 'If there's anything you want you must come to me. I want you to promise.'

Beneath his darkly compelling gaze she moved uneasily. 'I'm sure I won't need anything you haven't already provided. Your home is very comfortable, Max.'

'Do you like it?' His voice was harsh yet eager, as if, against his better judgment, her answer was important to him.

'It would be difficult not to,' she replied wryly.

He moved nearer, until she could almost feel his breath on her face, and cravenly she tried to move back. Once more, though, an electric current seemed to link them, making her legs incapable of movement as it lanced through her. 'Has Deirdre said anything to disturb you?' he frowned, searching the rather anxious lines of her face.

'Of course not,' Selena gulped. 'Your sister is very good.'

'She's paid to be.'

Impatiently, Selena tore her gaze from his. How typical of him! Max Heger would take it for granted anything could be bought with money.

'All the same, I appreciate her kindness.'

'Ah, yes,' he sneered, 'I was forgetting how appreciative you can be.'

Startled, she looked quickly at him, knowing there
was more to what he said than was obvious, but before
she could challenge him, he turned to leave her.

'I'll see you downstairs, Selena. After lunch I'll show
you over the rest of the house and grounds. You never
know, you could be spending a lot of time here in the
very near future, and then there's your new career to
discuss.'

'You know how I feel about that, Max.'

'You don't have to look so worried,' he smiled
grimly. 'I'm going to devote the whole weekend to
making you change your mind.'

No sooner had he gone than Pearl arrived.

'Oh, no!' Selena exclaimed, without thinking. 'If you
won't give me a minute I'll never be ready. And all I
want to do is wash my hands.'

'Carry on, then, don't mind me.' Frowning, Pearl
dropped into the nearest chair. 'What was Max doing
here?'

'You saw him?'

'Don't look so surprised. I nearly fell over him, yet he
didn't see me.'

Under the circumstances, there would be no use
denying it. Glumly Selena sighed. 'Apparently satisfying
himself that I was comfortable while ostensibly taking
another opportunity to threaten me.'

'Then there's no need for me to do it.' With a delicate
yawn, Pearl rose to her feet to precede Selena from the
room.

Deirdre's husband, Kit Ryde, appeared for lunch. He
was a quiet man with a rather brooding air about him
which suggested to Selena that he wasn't altogether
happy with his life. He was pleasant and courteous and
he and Max seemed to get on well enough. He was so
charming to Pearl that before long Selena decided her
first impression had been wrong. Sitting a little away
from his wife, Kit could be almost seen to relax.
Deirdre, Selena though, would take a lot of living up to,

being almost as high-powered as her brother.

'Don't tire Selena out too much—remember my
dinner party,' she warned Max after coffee, when he
announced his intention of showing Selena around. She
went on to say, as she saw Selena glance quickly at
Pearl, that Miss Burnett had already agreed to come
with her to help open a local autumn bazaar. Everyone
would be delighted, as Miss Burnett was very well
known, more especially after her part in the popular TV
series which had just finished.

Naturally this appealed to Pearl more than spending
the afternoon tramping in damp woods. Selena, although she had no real desire to bask in Pearl's reflected glory, would rather have gone to the bazaar, if
she had been given a choice—which she was not. As
Max took hold of her arm, firmly drawing her away
from the others, she knew she would enjoy walking with
him around his estate better than anything else. It was
when he began trying to persuade her to become an
actress that her pleasure would fade.

He didn't broach the subject until he had shown her
most of the property, both inside and out. It was impressive and she could see he expected her to be impressed. The house itself was large and rambled endear-
ingly, with the nursery wing being entirely independent
from the rest of it.

'Deirdre's idea, not mine,' Max shrugged. 'For all she
likes to give the opposite impression, she likes the children where they can neither be seen or heard.'

This reminded Selena so much of her own parents
that she gave a visible start.

Thinking she was merely surprised at his sister's
unmaternal attitude, Mac continued, 'If I ever marry
I'll want children too, but I'd want them where I could
both see and hear them.'

'Children shouldn't be tucked away and only brought
out at convenient moments,' Selena agreed. 'I wouldn't
want that either, and I hope to have a couple.

Fortunately the average husband can't afford a household where it's possible to keep children out of sight.'

Wouldn't you be nervous about having a child?' Max's face hardened suddenly, so revengefully that she felt a flicker of unaccountable apprehension.

'I suppose I might be, a little.' She felt an odd reluctance to discuss such an intimate subject casually and faltered over her reply. 'It—it must be quite an experience.'

'Experience?' he drawled mockingly. 'That's something you're busy collecting, I believe?'

Why should he think so? His thoughts leapt so quickly Selena could never hope to keep up with him. This time she didn't even try but merely retorted, 'Why not?' with as indifferent a shrug as she could manage. Let him look briefly incensed. What she did with her life was entirely her own business!

Silently he steered her out of doors in the direction of a huge heated swimming pool. Glancing up at his still grim face, she had an uneasy conviction that he would have liked to have picked her up and thrown her in. Hastily, she moved on. There were tennis courts, then larger areas of land given over to lawns and shrubs. The shrubs, Max told her, were easier to maintain than flower beds, at a time when good gardeners were almost a thing of the past. Only the beds in the immediate vicinity of the houses were kept up, and these were mostly herbaceous.

'Will your sister and her husband always live here?' she asked, after they had wandered some distance across the nearby fields and then paused to turn and consider the beautiful setting of the house.

'Deirdre would like to, but Kit is keen to go back to America. He only came here to oblige me, as I've had to spend most of the last few years in the States. At the moment it's only under discussion, but I believe they'll finish up there permanently.'

'The children seem darlings,' commented Selena.

'They are. And I think it's important that their future is settled before they're much older.'

He seemed genuinely concerned. Somehow she hadn't thought of him as a man who would be interested in children. What he said now, and his remarks in the house, seemed to confirm that he was.

'I hope I see more of them while I'm here?' she said wistfully.

'I'd rather have your undivided attention,' he said.

He spoke so firmly that she was sure he was about to bring up the very subject she was dreading, and she broke in quickly. 'Will you ever live here for long periods yourself?'

'I'm considering it,' he surprised her by saying. 'After my next film I'm thinking of retiring to write. It's not just an idea,' he said dryly, noticing her rather incredulous expression. 'I've already had four books published over the years, but I've never had time to devote myself to writing as I'd like to.'

'I'm sorry,' Selena apologised, 'I didn't mean to suggest you aren't serious, it's just that I thought making films was more important to you than anything else.'

'It was,' he regarded her with a kind of coldness she found disturbing, 'but not any more. A lot of things have changed—are changing,' he added, as if he didn't altogether care for what he saw. 'Nothing for the better, as far as I can see, but there it is.'

How could he expect her to understand what he didn't seem able to himself? One thing did seem clear, though, and she felt her heart lighten with relief. 'So this final film you're making won't really matter very much?'

'Of course it will,' he returned so sharply she went hot with embarrassment. 'I'm a perfectionist, Selena. I like everything I touch to be as near perfect as possible.'

Taking a deep breath, she forced herself to be brave, unable to bear the suspense. For hours she had been trying to avoid the subject, now she knew she couldn't any longer. 'Surely it can't really matter whether I'm in your new film or not, especially as it's to be your last one?'

'It does matter,' he replied, with what she sensed was deliberate slowness, 'otherwise I wouldn't have asked you.'

Wishing angrily that she had never mentioned her own involvement, she tried quickly to talk of something else. 'Won't you miss all the activity? This will be an entirely different way of life.'

'Living here?' His brows rose. 'I don't intend becoming a recluse, if that's what you mean. I expect I shall still travel quite a bit. Who knows,' he teased, staring at her intently, 'you might even be prepared to come with me occasionally?'

Selena sighed. When he talked like this she didn't take him seriously, but she wished he wouldn't. She had little doubt that if she didn't accompany him on his travels some other woman would. And this hurt, more than she cared to admit. Again she tried to deny that she could be falling in love with him. There might be something between them but she doubted it could be this.

'Come,' Max said lightly, drawing her gently towards a green copse a few yards away, at the other side of the parklands, 'if you aren't absolutely gasping for a cup of tea, let's sit down and talk for a while. I'll promise not to make love to you.'

Pink tinted her cheeks as she tried to protest, as he pushed her down on the dry autumn bracken. It crackled under their weight and a lone wasp they disturbed flew away with a protesting buzz. The sun shone through the trees and the air was warm here, where it was sheltered, even in late October. Selena could smell the sharp scent of the pine trees, see the red berries of the rowan and hear the gentle wind moving with autumnal sadness through the branches.

'Like Kipling said,' Max murmured softly, breaking a

short silence with lazy reluctance, 'your English summer's done.'

'Sometimes it lingers quite a while,' she smiled, glancing around her appreciatively. Then, more anxiously, 'We won't have to stay too long.'

'If you're worrying about Deirdre's dinner party, we'll be back in plenty of time.' Wryly he propped himself on an elbow, watching her idly. 'I come to Lynton to escape that kind of thing, but Deirdre never learns.'

'She might find it dull here if she didn't entertain. So might you, if you came to live here permanently.'

Denying this, he shook his dark head. 'The pace is different, but this is what I like, what I need. Something slower, not quite so urgent. Do you find the country dull, Selena?'

'No, but then I've always loved it. The school I went to was surrounded by green fields and I would much rather have spent my holidays there than in London.'

'You're not a schoolgirl now, though.'

Feeling she had already betrayed too much of her real self, she swung irrationally to try and cover up. 'Oh, I find lots to compensate in the city. There are plenty of people willing to help a girl enjoy herself in London.'

'I can imagine,' he replied, with a grimness she thought was uncalled for. She must be a better actress than she thought, if he believed everything she said.

To her dismay, almost as if a signal had passed from her mind to his, he shrugged and began telling her what her life would be like if she joined his film company and became an actress for a while. He made it sound all very interesting, even rewarding, and the part he described seemed quite within the range of even the most modest capabilities, but even so, Selena still shook her head.

'Wait until tomorrow,' he urged, again refusing to accept an outright refusal.

She was surprised that he was always granting her more time, and that he continued to want her. So much for her hopes that this weekend might end his desire to have her with him. If anything his determination appeared to be increasing. Yet she was ashamed to find herself agreeing to think about it, taking a coward's way out. How could she explain that she was doing it only for Pearl's sake? He wouldn't understand.

'I'd look after you,' he promised, taking a strand of her silky hair and wrapping it several times around one of his fingers. 'You wouldn't be at the mercy of every man who took a fancy to you. I'd personally see to it that you were quite safe.'

How safe would that be? Uneasily, her heart racing as he played with her bright hair, she glanced at him, the question very readable in her blue eyes.

Softly Max laughed—she could see very sure of ultimate victory. 'As safe as you want to be?' he suggested.

'Look——' she began, then cried out as unwisely she jerked her head. Tears of pain springing to her eyes, she challenged him, 'What sort of a role are you really asking me to play?'

'Oh, come,' he grinned wickedly, 'surely you don't think I would go to such elaborate lengths just to seduce a girl?'

'I wouldn't put anything past you!'

'Ah,' he sighed, his eyes glinting in mock seriousness, 'I'd like to be the first man in your life, Selena. What would you say to that?'

Desperately she strove to keep the atmosphere light. If he continued, as he was doing, she could soon be a little helpless heap at his feet! 'I'm afraid you can't be,' she forced a careless laugh. 'I've promised someone else.'

Who? Amazed at her own duplicity, she tried wildly to conjure up a man's name, in case Max asked. Fortunately he didn't. Her spark of inspiration—or was it imagination?—appeared to have worked, better than she would have thought possible. Max was staring at her with actual dislike, as if he believed every word she had uttered.

'You still have time to change your mind,' he said curtly, dropping a punishing kiss on her startled lips before releasing her.

For a long moment, as he jumped to his feet, pulling her up with him, she wished she had been able to. It would be so easy to give in to him, whatever that might involve. It was only because she felt instinctively that it might involve more than she was prepared to give that she hesitated.

As they strolled silently back to the house, the brief pressure of Max's mouth on hers lingered, filling her with a suddenly restless desire for more, a desire which she tried hard but unsuccessfully to ignore.

During the dinner party that followed, Max didn't stray far from her side, for all she felt he was still annoyed with her. Selena could only believe he imagined he was protecting a business deal he wasn't yet sure of.

Because the evenings were growing distinctly chilly, Selena had brought a long velvet skirt which she wore on this occasion with a matching top, in a fine, almost see-through material. Before coming downstairs she had brushed her hair until it fell in heavy burnished waves to her slim shoulders and made up her face carefully. While the results might not be quite up to Pearl's standards, Selena felt quite pleased by the time she had finished. She was aware that she was looking nice, if not quite as sophisticated as she had looked when she and Pearl had dined with Max in London.

Before her other guests arrived, Deirdre had explained that this was a dinner party Max had previously avoided, and that most of those coming tonight had received their invitations only yesterday morning, after Max had rung from London to say he would be down.

'Most of them can't imagine anything more exciting

and glamorous than a real live film director,' she laughed.

Max groaned. 'Next time,' he threatened, 'I won't tell you I'm coming. I'll just arrive.'

'If Kit and I stay in the States, as I think we've almost decided to, we won't be here, so you'll have an excuse to avoid entertaining,' she teased back.

'Unless I can find someone else to do it for me,' he glanced with apparent innocence at Selena. 'I might find myself a hostess, if only temporarily.'

'Don't count on me!' she hissed, in soft undertones, as he wandered over to where she sat, his brows still slightly raised.

He sat down on the arm of her chair, which must have emphasised his intentions even more. 'Man could never survive without hope,' he drawled, his eyes lingering over her closely.

He appeared to have no compunction about letting her see he continued to hope as the evening wore on. Nor during the following morning, when he came to her bedroom, followed by his niece and two young nephews. She wasn't aware he was there until she heard him call her name, and when she blinked in startled surprise he told her she must get up as they were all going swimming.

'But I haven't brought a suit!' she protested, sitting straight up in bed and, like a child, scarcely bothering to hide a prodigious yawn. The party had gone on until the early hours and she had proved very popular. She had danced a lot, mostly with Max, for he had been oddly reluctant to let another man near her. This morning she thought the effort of trying to avoid him must have exhausted her, for she still felt tired.

'I'd rather stay here,' she smiled at him sleepily.

'So would I—if I could be in there with you,' he grinned.

'Which is the kind of remark you might feel compelled to make, even if I were a hundred,' she muttered unevenly.

'I'm not all that devoted to pretty speeches,' he growled impatiently. 'Have you any idea how you look? Shall I send the kids back to their own quarters?'

'No! Don't be silly. They wouldn't understand.' She had forgotten to pull the sheet up to her chin and her satin nightdress was no protection from predatory male eyes, but she refused to imitate the blushing females in books by diving under the bedclothes. It did, though, take a lot of courage to brazen it out, for although Max kept his distance, she felt he didn't miss a thing.

The children, who had contented themselves so far with playing games in the corridor, now became curious. 'Is she coming, Uncle Max?' enquired the little girl.

'Are you?' he joined his own query to theirs.

'I've nothing to wear!' Selena was impatient that she had to tell him again.

'You can borrow a costume from the changing room by the pool,' he said. 'Deirdre's friends are always leaving them. Every now and again I believe she sends a pile to a local jumble sale.'

'Then I will, if you'll get out,' Selena gave in.

'Must I?'

'For the children's sake, Mr Heger,' she retorted with mock severity, wondering how she came to be flirting almost blatantly with a man she didn't even approve of.

The pool was warm, but if it hadn't been Selena's bikini wouldn't have helped her. The only one she could find to fit left nothing much to the imagination. The children didn't notice, however. If they had had their own way they would have swum naked, but after Max laughingly turned thumbs down to that, they emerged from the changing rooms very properly attired.

Max himself wore black trunks and Selena felt her eyes riveted as he strode towards her. She hadn't been prepared for the effect of his tall, well-proportioned body, and her eyes widened, with a helplessness that reddened her cheeks, over his long legs and powerful thighs to his broad, bare shoulders. Wishing fervently that she had stayed in her room, she sucked in her breath unsteadily. She wobbled, taking an instinctive step backwards, and fell right into the deep end.

Hearing a splash, as she emerged half drowned, she felt rather than saw him beside her.

'Whatever made you fall in like that?' he asked, with aggravating coolness, and a slight smile.

As if he didn't guess! Still spluttering, Selena shivered miserably, rubbing the excess water from her face and eyes. As she lowered her arm it came in contact with his wet, hair-covered chest and she jerked back with an audible wince. 'I didn't realise I was so near the edge,' she whispered.

His gaze levelled on her steadily, his mouth quirking with a faint amusement as he noted her air of bemusement. 'I know what's wrong with you, you're missing your early morning cup of tea. Come on,' firmly he caught hold of her hand, drawing her out of the pool with him. 'It's a good job I happened to order some before we came out, and I see one of the maids has just arrived with it now.'

CHAPTER FIVE

WHILE Selena was grateful for anything that might make her feel better, she would rather she hadn't had to acknowledge Max Heger's thoughtfulness. Not that he appeared to expect a lot of appreciation, and she realised he would be more used to girls like Pearl who took this sort of thing entirely for granted. She enjoyed the hot tea and biscuits so much she was inclined to dawdle over it, quite content to sit idly listening to the children chattering like small magpies as they, in turn, drank their orange juice.

It was quite clear that they adored their uncle, and his warm tolerance with them suggested he returned their affection. Selena pondered over this as she swam, while he entertained them in their own small pool. He was a man who obviously had two distinct sides to his personality. The warm, caring side was the one his immediate family would mostly see, the harder, ruthless vitality underneath would be kept for the business side of his life. And she'd be a fool to imagine there wasn't a sensuous side as well, but this Selena didn't want to think about.

After she had circled the pool several times she climbed out and played with the children while Max had his turn. She found herself thinking wistfully that it might have been nice if they could have swam together, but he didn't ask her to come in with him, and of course the children couldn't be left unsupervised. A little later she helped them get dressed, as the youngest boy, James, insisted, when away from the eagle eye of his nurse, on putting everything on the wrong way around. So much laughter ensued over this that Max, approaching them wryly, declared that if they didn't hurry up they would miss breakfast. In spite of this, Selena was quite sorry to see them trotting off to their nursery.

In the dining-room, Max glanced at her thoughtfully. 'You seem to be very fond of children, Selena?'

'Yes,' she was so hungry she didn't pause to consider her reply, 'I was always good with the younger ones at school. Perhaps I should have trained as a children's nurse or gone in for teaching. I still could . . .'

'If?'

'If . . . Oh, I see.' Her confusion was concealed behind long lashes as she blinked at him. She was surprised that he wanted to know. 'If I could get myself properly sorted out, I suppose. I did think about it, but as a children's nurse I wouldn't have had much freedom.'

'And this is important to you?'

Max sounded so suddenly, coldly angry that she found herself blinking at him again. How could she make him understand, without going into long boring explanations, that after leaving school freedom had seemed more important to her than anything else? 'Isn't it important to everyone?' she countered carelessly.

His mouth merely tightened. 'How about your parents?'

'I rarely see them.'

'You feel sorry for yourself because of this?'

'No!' but she paused briefly over her delicious plateful of bacon and eggs.

He didn't seem to notice her reflective frown. 'You consider it a blessing in disguise, perhaps?'

Becoming aware of his condemning tone, she resented it. 'Sometimes,' she agreed tensely, thinking of her mother and stepfather's last visit when they had quarrelled loudly and bitterly most of the time, ignoring Selena whom they had supposedly come to see. Still, that had been over a year ago, and she'd been only eighteen and a bit. Since then she had grown up completely and it didn't hurt so much any more. Max's mouth clamped, as though he restrained other, more withering comments. Curtly he refilled her coffee cup and passed the toastrack and marmalade. 'I often get the impression,' he said enigmatically, 'that the modern girl grows up far too soon. Have you ever thought of spreading your wings, seeing the world?' he asked abruptly.

Carefully Selena spread golden butter on a piece of hot toast. 'I'd have to make some money first. At the moment I can't make enough to afford a place of my own, even to share with someone.'

His face hardened. 'Ah, that! The ultimate goal of the young. Absolute independence and sexual freedom.'

'Well, there must be worse things to aim for.' She didn't want to discuss sexual freedom with him—or any other man—so she ignored that.

'It palls, believe me,' he said cynically. 'This is why I'm suggesting that a role in my film would be ideal for your first real venture. It would be an adventure and you'd gain experience, while I'd be there to protect you.'

'No—no, thank you.' Her appetite suddenly gone, she pushed her last bit of toast away. Why must he always return to this? Always, just when friendship between them seemed possible, he had to spoil it by trying to make her change her mind. 'I'm sorry,' she reiterated. She had meant to wait, but all at once she was conscious of being sick and uneasy about continuing such a deception. Bravely she tried to meet his calculating eyes. 'It's no use, and you'll have to accept it. I just don't want to be a film star, not even a minor one. I'm sorry, Max, but there it is, I can't pretend any longer.' Anxiously she added, 'I suppose you wouldn't consider saying nothing to Pearl until tomorrow?'

'Why not until then?'

Nervously Selena swallowed. 'If—well, when Pearl is annoyed she can be embarrassingly frank.'

'And will she be annoyed if she has to look elsewhere for work?' he asked.

'Furious!' Unconsciously, Selena shuddered.

'Naturally I'll wait,' Max assured her smoothly, 'if it will make you any happier.'

Slowly she nodded, her confused eyes fixed on his sardonic face. Having expected a roar of anger, she found herself trembling with relief. Max didn't seem so very disturbed by her final refusal, after all. In fact, as she continued to stare at him in some bewilderment, he merely picked up one of the morning papers and began to read.

Not sure what to think, she was relieved when Kit and Deirdre appeared almost simultaneously and the conversation became general. Pearl, it appeared, was having her usual lemon juice and black coffee in bed.

What would Pearl say when she heard she wasn't going to get the part?—and Max's attitude was quite uncompromising about that. Of course there were other films and shows. One disappointment wasn't going to mean the end of Pearl's career, and Pearl was well used to them. Something else was bound to turn up very soon.

If Max was disappointed in Selena he managed to disguise his feelings successfully. After breakfast he went out riding with Kit, again seeming to demonstrate his superb physical fitness, but the rest of the day he devoted to his sister and his two guests. Sensing that Pearl was getting impatiently curious as the day wore on, Selena did her best to avoid her, which wasn't too difficult as Max was continually between them.

After dinner he surprised everyone, including Selena, by announcing that he was taking Selena out for a drink, and advised the others not to wait up as they might be late.

'Just the two of us,' he said, smiling down on her, and she felt vaguely anxious that he might unwittingly give the impression that they were interested in each other. Pearl, she could see, for all she was enjoying the luxurious comforts of this country house, would liked to have come along with them, but Max didn't issue an invitation.

At a loss as to what he could want to say to her, Selena obligingly ran to fetch her coat, but it wasn't until they were seated in the almost deserted lounge of a quiet hotel many miles away that he condescended to enlighten her.

After ordering their drinks he waited until they arrived, all the time studying her pensive face. A swift glance at him revealed him mulling over a question of some importance, and Selena turned away, her cheeks growing hot. Why was it, she wondered despairingly, that he could so easily stir her? She was sure he was aware of this and sometimes did it deliberately.

Taking pity on her at last, he said, 'If you won't agree to being Pearl's maid in a film, Selena, would you be interested in being nursemaid to Deirdre's infants on their trip to the States?'

So startled was Selena by this suggestion that she was struck dumb. A trip to the States! On the face of it, it might seem a wonderful opportunity, but it would mean seeing a lot of Max. Wordlessly she stared at him. This in itself was a danger she would rather not contemplate. And then there was Ronald. How could she possibly let him down?

Quickly she lowered her eyes, as her gaze threatened to become locked with his for ever. 'I can't believe you're serious.' She hesitated uncertainly before refusing. Hadn't he proved himself quite capable of passing an idle remark simply to tease her, and she had no wish to make a fool of herself. 'I can't believe you are,' she repeated, with a nervous little laugh which almost betrayed the unsteady state of her heart.

His wide firm mouth pursed with a slight impatience. 'I wouldn't have made such a suggestion if I were not.'

'No, I suppose not,' still hesitating, she frowned, 'but why me?'

'Why not?' he confounded her with the unanswerable, his manner crisp, indicating that he was more than well equipped to deal with any number of similar objections.

For a long moment Selena twisted her glass of sherry uneasily in her slender fingers. It might have helped her more if she drank it, but she felt unable suddenly to even raise it to her lips. This evening she had no idea how lovely she looked. She was wearing a dress in a soft shade of pink and had painted her nails and mouth in a slightly paler shade of the same colour. With her glossy hair and pale skin she looked like a study in beautiful pastels, and she heard the man by her side draw in his breath. This, though the reason for it wasn't clear to her, brought her eyes back to his face.

With some difficulty she said, 'I know you must think I'm mad to turn down such a chance—and I must, but among other things, I have a—a certain commitment, a promise I have to keep.'

Max's head jerked so sharply at this, her uneasiness increased, and she paused in the middle of her somewhat muddled explanations. Narrowly his glance wandered. He appeared to be concentrating on a party just leaving, but she felt instinctively he didn't see them. The rigid angle of his averted head suddenly lanced her with fright.

'It—it's not that important that I go, is it?' she gulped, hoping he wasn't going to be too angry.

His mouth curving with a bewildering cynicism, he glanced at her again. 'Perhaps I should explain more fully. If you can bear to put your—er—commitments to one side for a moment? I intend flying to the States with Deirdre and Kit and the children tomorrow afternoon. I have houses and several apartments over there. You would be living in luxury with very little to do.'

'But you asked me to go as nursemaid,' she quavered, slightly incredulous that he could describe looking after three children as having little to do.

'Until we get there, it will provide as good an excuse as any as to why you should be with us,' he enlightened her suavely. 'Actually the nanny the children have now is leaving, as Kit and Deirdre have decided to remain in the States permanently, and while Deirdre has already arranged to engage someone else over there, you can always help out occasionally. It might be a chance to find out if you'd really like to make a career of looking after other people's offspring. Whatever you do you'd be there at least a month, as I have an extremely full schedule to get through before we return. Mind you, I won't be completely tied up. I'll make sure you have a good time.'

Somehow the more he said the more hurt she became, without really knowing why. Weakly she protested, 'You couldn't expect anyone to go at such short notice! I'd have to go back to London.'

'It can't be necessary.' There was a steely hardness in his eyes as he prepared systematically to dispose of her arguments. 'You won't be able to before we leave. We will go there, but only to catch the plane.'

'No! Please stop!' Wildly Selena jumped to her feet, feeling completely battered by the strength of his determination. 'It's not possible, I tell you. Besides, I don't want to!'

'Of course you do!' Eyes glittering with rage, his hand flashed out to grasp her wrist. 'What the devil's got into you, Selena? For any girl it's the chance of a lifetime.'

Why did Pearl's words suddenly come back to her? 'Max Heger won't ask you to live with him, or marry him. He just waits until a girl falls into his arms, with little apparent encouragement on his part.' Pearl had undoubtedly known what she was talking about, and she'd do well to remember it!

'I'm sorry, Mr Heger.' Selena's voice trembled and her wrist, in his cruel grip was beginning to ache, but whatever happened he must be made to understand that she wouldn't give in. She had no intention of agreeing to his proposal, enticing though it might be. Yet it wasn't easy to stiffen her resolve, with his breath hot on her cold cheeks as he jerked her down beside him again, his eyes burning her up.

'I can't go.' She clung to her decision stubbornly, trying to close her mind to his dark attraction. 'I won't go, and that's that! Hasn't anyone ever said no to you before?'

'My ego isn't as inflated as you apparently believe,' he rapped. 'Perhaps you should be taking a look at your own? At least your manners.'

Realising he could be right, Selena bit her lip hard. She had been impertinent, but she wouldn't apologise, for hadn't he provoked her? 'I've had no complaints so far about my manners,' she cried angrily. 'Just because I choose to remain in London and—and spend my time with someone else, it doesn't mean I'm uncouth!'

His voice cracking with ice, he asked, 'So you intend keeping your—your promises?'

'Naturally.' Believing he was referring to her work, she answered loftily.

Cruelly Max pulled her nearer, and she thought he might have injured her arm, for she heard a faint crack. He didn't even bother to say he was sorry, when he saw her rubbing it, and the pain was fleetingly reflected in the delicate lines of her face.

'I don't understand you.' Curtly he waved away a curious barman who came to enquire if Max wanted to order more drinks. 'When I first got to know you, I thought we had a lot in common, that in some way we clicked. I offered you a job, though, because you seemed just what I was looking for, but you turned it down, even when it meant hurting your cousin. Then I invite you to America, all expenses paid, and you turn up that snooty little nose of yours even higher. And it's not because you dislike me. I don't think it's that at all. So what is it?'

As incensed as he was now, she cried, 'You can try shaking an answer out of me, but it mightn't be the one you expect.'

'Anything's worth trying,' he retaliated harshly. 'You put ideas into my head.' Taking her at her word, he slid his hands to her shoulders and shook her until she gasped for breath.

'Stop it!' Her raised voice brought the barman back, which forced Max to let her go. Quite indifferent to the paleness of her face, her ordered another whisky for himself but nothing for her, and when the man brought it for him he tossed him a five-pound note, telling him to keep the change.

'What was that for—silence money?' Selena jeered, almost in tears. 'In case he might be tempted to whisper it around that the great Max Heger tries to browbeat people into doing what he wants?'

'You little vixen!' Smouldering, he swallowed his whisky in one go, as if it were water. Standing up, he yanked her to her feet. 'Let's get out of here,' he snarled, 'before I'm tempted to do something worse than shake you!'

Selena didn't know which was aching most, her shoulders or her heart, but in a way she was grateful for their quarrel as it certainly seemed to have put a lot of distance between them. Or so she thought!

In the car, in the darkened car park, Max didn't give her a chance to calm down and collect her senses. Turning, as swiftly as he closed the door, he dragged her to him. Without warning his mouth descended to crush her lips, forcing them apart with such cruel precision it knocked the breath right out of her.

Mind-spinning moments later, he lifted his head to rasp against her throbbing mouth, 'Don't I deserve something by way of compensation? I've provided you with a free weekend and all you've done is waste my time. All right, I knew what I was doing, but, by heavens, so did you! You never had any intention of taking that part, had you?'

'No, I had not!' she agreed shrilly, her lips, when they did manage to move, producing an effect quite the opposite from that which she strove for. She sounded rudely uncaring when, in fact, it had only been to help Pearl that she had come at all.

'You're a practised little deceiver,' Max grated, 'An unrepentant one at that, but at least I've forced you to admit it.'

What use to deny it when he was convinced she was to blame for everything? Yet the true blame for what had happened must surely lie with him more than anyone else? Defiantly she stared at him. 'I'll only admit that I'm glad I refused to have anything more to do with you.'

'You'll live to regret it.'

The hard fury in his eyes frightened her. She twisted in a renewed attempt to escape him. 'Let me go!' she cried. 'You must be out of your mind!'

'And I'll make sure you're out of yours, before I'm through!' he exclaimed, leashed fury in his tones as his mouth came down on hers again, to ravage it.

Seconds ago she had thought she was too numb with despair to feel anything, and it was with shocked surprise that, as he crushed her against him, she felt herself beginning to respond. Before she could prevent it, parts of her body went weak and began pushing closer to the hardness of his, appearing to have a will of their own. As flames reminiscent of a forest fire out of control started racing through her, she made a desperate effort to tear herself from his demanding arms and mouth. Bringing her hand up, she tried to edge back a little, intending to increase this advantage by slapping or clawing his face. Unfortunately her clenched hands refused to uncurl in time. Consequently it was her doubled fist that hit him a resounding blow over his eye.

With a sharp expression of pain which startled her to a full realisation of what she had done, Max let her go.

Rapidly he disposed of her instant remorse with a few bitten-off remarks not especially designed to soothe any girl's sensitive ears.

Ignoring her shaken figure, crouched away from him as far as she could get, he ripped the car from the gravelled yard with such a screech of tyres it mercifully drowned the scathing denouncement of her still flowing harshly from his lips.

When at last his icy observations came to an end no further word was exchanged between them until they arrived at Lynton, where Selena managed a tortured but extremely cold goodnight. She hoped never to have to see him again. She didn't know how she was to get back to London, but it wouldn't be with him!

Apparently the family had taken Max at his word and retired, as there was no one around. All but the hall lights had obviously been extinguished. Everyone, tired out by the festivities of the previous evening, had seemingly taken to their beds.

Relieved at being spared the further strain of making polite conversation when feeling so dangerously near to breaking down, Selena ignored Max and almost ran upstairs. If it had been possible she would have left Lynton immediately, but distraught as she was, she recognised the folly of wandering on strange country roads in the middle of a dark autumn night. Even so, she was so taut she felt like screaming. She didn't know why she was still gripped by the scene which had just taken place in Max's car. In a terribly unnerving way she had a feeling that she and Max had become one, instead of two separate entities, which even her rather childish reactions had failed to tear apart.

In her room she tore off her clothes and dived under the shower, hoping somehow that this would make her believe she belonged to herself again. Hastily she dried her wet body, but she was still shivering so hard it took time. Had she been a fool, turning down Max's offer? A whole month in the States, looked after by a man like him, being pampered and probably made love to by him? Yes—or no? The two words struggled for supremacy in her overwrought mind until they seemed to burn her.

'Oh, damn!' she cried aloud, then repeated it, something she had never done before. It brought her to her senses with a jerk, making her frighteningly aware of how much she was disturbed. Half sobbing, in an effort to pull herself together, she wrapped herself in a huge warm towel. The heat penetrated her cold limbs, bringing an odd comfort, and also helped soothe her tormented thoughts. Hugging the towel closer, she returned to the bedroom.

To her dismay, just as she had managed to untangle and comb her long silky hair, the door opened and Max strode in. 'Oh, no . . .!' she didn't know she moaned aloud in despair. Why had she forgotten to turn the key?

Max didn't, though. He turned it, then slipped it into his pocket, while Selena froze to complete stillness.

Conscious of how she must look, and above all what his action might denote, she gasped, 'Will you get out!'

'No.' He stared down at her, anger still glinting in his eyes along with a reluctant appreciation of her smooth white shoulders and slender, towel-clad body, 'I want to talk to you.'

She ignored this, for she was sure they had nothing left to say to each other. Nothing had changed and they were both still angry. Anything more would serve no useful purpose. In mute protest she spread her slim, expressive fingers. 'You'd better go at once. What if your sister hears?'

'She won't,' he drawled. 'She and Kit have their own wing upstairs. This is my own private one, for the exclusive use of myself and my guests, but even Pearl is too far away to be within earshot.'

Selena's eyes widened with contemptuous astonishment, which would have goaded a lesser man. Ignoring the hardening cast of his face, she attempted to adopt a scornfully belligerent manner. It might be her only chance. It would never do to cower in front of such a man. 'I don't know what arrangements you usually have with your guests,' she said coldly, voicing an obvious disdain, 'but I have no wish to be included. Kindly leave my room!'

Little did she realise that the aloof sophistication she strove after, which desperation and a too rapidly beating heart drove her to affect, was going to produce entirely different results from those she had hoped for.

Max, as Selena's attitude continued to incense, made no attempt to do as she asked. His demeanour if anything hardened, and he obviously didn't bother to wonder at the intense pallor on her face which betrayed that she was far from as confident as her sharp words suggested.

'I'll go when I'm ready,' he replied smoothly. 'The time of my departure might actually rest with you. I told you I want to talk.'

'Well, I don't!' Fright, and the miserable knowledge that she was fast becoming far too attracted towards a man she scarcely knew, stiffened her resolve to something near hysteria. 'Look,' she hissed, 'I don't want to see you or hear you, and if you don't get out I'll—I'll...'

'Yes, Miss North?' he prompted softly, when as she wondered how best she could threaten him, her voice trailed off.

His tone might have warned her to slow up, but she was such a mass of shaking nerves nothing else could get through. 'You don't think I don't know how to look after myself, do you?'

'Oh,' his laughter was little short of insulting, 'I'm quite sure you do, but not in a bedroom.'

For a second Selena clutched her slipping towel with visible apprehension. Then fearing she had abjectly betrayed herself, she cried recklessly, 'A state of affairs I

can rectify any time I want. In fact . . .' About to invent
a more unlikely story, she stopped in time, horrified by
the lengths she was allowing Max to goad her to.

'Yes——? In fact what, Selena?'

'It's none of your business,' she attempted to brazen
it out.

'But I can guess,' he sneered softly, while a hard fury
turned his eyes to ice. For a long moment he considered
her closely, not apparently trusting himself to speak.
Coolly he asked, as though driven to it, 'Are you in
love?'

In love? Surely he hadn't guessed how she felt about
him? Fear lay behind her emphatic reply. 'Of course
not!'

'So,' he sneered, contemptuously, 'you're going into
this with your eyes wide open? Just an experiment?'

What was he talking about? Why was he so furious?
He was white with anger now. It must have been
mounting all evening to have reached such a peak.
There was a curious grimness to his face as he advanced
towards her, a determination full of hardening intent. 'I
don't know what you mean.' She retreated a step.

'You're spending tomorrow night with another man,
I believe? You promised.'

Pearl must have told him she had promised to work
for Ronald, which surely should have convinced him
she was telling the truth about having commitments.
'It's none of your business,' she repeated heatedly, 'but
yes, I am!'

His mouth tightened and his eyes were insolent now
as they went over her. 'A towel is the most deceptive
garment. What else around a woman could arouse such
intimate speculation for the price?'

'Go—go away!' She became alarmed, as she sensed
for some reason that he was barely under control, and
that for Max Heger it would take something of some
magnitude to drive him to such a pitch. As his hands
reached out she swiftly slapped them away, but, as this

brought sudden recall, her eyes leapt to his face. Close, she could see the beginnings of a large purple bruise over his cheekbone, where her fist had caught him, and she gasped.

His temper simmering to boiling point, he taunted, 'Yes, take a good look, Selena, but if I have a beautiful black eye in the morning, I can guarantee you're going to hurt much more!'

As her breath caught apprehensively in her throat his expression reflected taut satisfaction. 'Before this night is out you'll certainly wish you hadn't turned down my offer. You still have time to consider going to America with me. That's what I came to ask you about.'

Selena was to wish agonisingly, over the next weeks, that she might have had the sense to agree to anything that might have got him out of her room before the worst happened. Unhappily she didn't believe he would dare do her any real harm and she failed to recognise the degree of danger until it was too late. Feeling confident that she could continue to defy him and get away with it, she replied fiercely,

'If this is a sample of what I can expect then I'm more than convinced I've made the right decision.'

Menacingly he rapped out, 'Yet you act in a way which seems to deny you're sure at all. Or is it that you're about as brave as the usual run of cowards, when it comes to the final showdown?'

Final showdown? Really frightened now, both by Max's words and manner, she made little attempt to conceal it. She recoiled from him as though he were evil. 'You'd better get out of here. You can apologise in the morning!'

As if this last challenge drove him beyond human limits, the tight curb he was obviously keeping on himself snapped. Suddenly aware of it, Selena felt her false courage disperse in a humiliating flash. Cravenly she began to beg, but it was doubtful if Max even heard the stammering pleas that fell from her lips as he grabbed

her and crushed her mouth brutally, with a smothered
exclamation, beneath his.

Now she had to fight both him and her own wavering
senses. Frantically she tried. Before his arms had a
chance to tighten, she lashed out, kicking and scratch-
ing, using her hands and feet, the only weapons at her
disposal, but even her most telling efforts had little
effect. As her hands encountered his hard muscles,
she was the one who suffered most, but eventually she
was defeated more by her own traitorous body than
anything else. Everything appeared to be working
against her—Max's strength, her own feminine weakness, and worst of all the chemistry which, even at a
touch, seemed capable of igniting between them with
shattering results.

At some time during her final struggles, she and the
towel she wore parted company, and she heard Max
mutter something hoarsely as he picked her up and carried her to the bed. As though his patience had departed with the last of his control, he threw her forcibly
on to the mattress. Badly dazed, with the breath
knocked completely out of her, Selena was forced to lie,
watching helplessly, as he ripped off his shirt and un-
buckled his belt. Then, after another pause, he was
beside her, throwing himself on top of her, his hands
knotting in her silky hair. As he held her fast, his mouth
reclaimed hers to resume a ruthless exploration. When,
in a last attempt, she tried feebly to escape him, his
other hand slid remorselessly around her waist, im-
prisoning her completely.

The sensuous movement of his lips burnt her like a
brand. Her heart began beating wildly, the passion
mounting between them telling her more than mere
words might have done. Max gave her no further chance
to express her fears, and long before his mouth eased
again she was beyond rational thinking. If anything
could have frightened her now, it might have been the
degree of her own response.

The hands which had been fighting him so fiercely now couldn't seem to hold him close enough. His warm mouth, moving softly over her face and neck, tormented her, while the roughness of his bare chest against her breasts filled her with a kind of painful delight. His heavy thigh lay over her own while his hard knee thrust her slim legs apart, but when she squirmed with startled virginal fright, the intensity of her own desire overwhelmed her. Wildly, forgetting restraint, she pressed nearer to him, until the heat of the blood racing through her veins was almost more than she could bear.

Very slightly, as he judged the exact degree of her surrender, Max raised himself, muttering gentle reassurances against her bruised and trembling lips. Selena was just a vortex of feeling, alive with frantic desire, and she didn't want to talk. When he gripped her delicate jaw, as if determined she should listen, she moved her head restlessly. Her ears were so dizzy she couldn't hear properly, but he seemed to be trying to explain something to her urgently. Softly, as he talked, the flat of his hand left her breasts to curve firmly on her narrow hips, his voice thick, as if he held his own passionate impatience on a tight rein only by exercising the greatest effort.

If he hadn't spoken Selena didn't think she would have realised what was happening until it was too late. While their bodies began fusing together and he murmured hoarsely about the joy of belonging to each other, a flash of enlightening fear seared right through her. Wildly trying to subdue a burning hunger to belong to him completely, she wrenched herself from his arms.

'Selena—for God's sake, we can't stop now!' Max's angry plea had little effect, but the force with which he brought her back to him had. The certain knowledge that her fate was sealed and she could no longer fight him set her body on fire while her head reeled.

Suddenly her senses were exploding in near shock, which might have found its equivalent in a major car accident. This, combined with the unfamiliar strain of the past hours, must have proved too much for her, for with a broken and surprised little cry, she found everything going black and knew no more.

Selena didn't recover consciousness until it was morning, when she awoke to find daylight streaming in through her bedroom window. For a moment she wasn't sure where she was and she lay frowning, only aware of her heavily aching head. Slowly she lifted a lethargic hand to push back her tumbled hair. She didn't usually suffer from headaches and she had felt all right when she'd gone to bed.

Until she had gone to bed! Suddenly, horrified, she sat up with a jerk, too immediately stunned to be aware of her nakedness. Everything came rushing back to her. Max had been here. They had fought and he had carried her to bed. Putting a hand over her racing heart, Selena forced herself to recall everything. He had made love to her. Or had they made love? With a mounting feeling of sickness she recalled how they had both wanted it. How their bodies and minds had been so perfectly attuned that nothing could have prevented it? Shivering with apprehension, she dropped her burning face in her hands. If only she could remember properly how it had ended!

CHAPTER SIX

WITH a kind of driven fury, Selena pressed tense hands against the sides of her throbbing head while her hair fell in a tumbled cloud about her shoulders. She did remember crying out, but she could also recall Max's voice raised in anger, and a weight descending on her which might have been Max or something else. 'Dear God!' she moaned, pushing back her long hair with frantic fingers. Where was Max now? What had he done?

Then, as she lifted a tear-stained, tormented face to stare around, as if the lonely, deserted room might supply the answer, her eyes fell on a letter propped against an ornament on the dressing-table. Shakily she scrambled out of bed to reach for it. It hadn't been there the evening before.

It was addressed to her. Taking hold of it with trembling fingers, she managed to tear it open. Inside was a piece of paper and a bundle of notes. There must have been several hundred pounds rolled up neatly inside a rubber band. When they fell from her numb fingers to the floor she carefully picked them up again, but laid them aside while she read what was written on the sheet of paper.

It was from Max. 'My dear Selena,' she read. 'Please accept the enclosed without hesitation. For me,' he went on cruelly, 'it would have been cheap at twice the price. I'm sure such a sum will help you to forgive me. If you still find it difficult try remembering how, in the first place, you intended giving yourself to a man you didn't love, after you returned to London. I heard you promise on the telephone, yourself. This being the case, I can't believe you can begrudge me being first. I'm sure there was a lot more between us than you will ever know with

96

another man, but at least I don't begrudge your boy-friend what's left. I've arranged for a car to take you and Pearl back to London, which will be less embar-rassing for both of us. Maybe we might meet again some day. Who knows? Max.'

A few hours later, in London, Pearl contributed further to Selena's misery, until she found it almost unbearable. All the way from Lynton Pearl had scarcely said a word. Now she more than made up for it.

Staring without sympathy at Selena's white face, she sneered sharply, 'I don't know what's been going on between you and Max this weekend, but it's not hard to guess!'

As she took a furious turn around the lounge in the penthouse, Selena watched her silently, still feeling ill from reaction.

'I'm out of the film!' Pearl halted abruptly in front of her again. 'I suppose you already know, though? Max told me early this morning. Which means you're out, too. I hope you understand?'

'Out?' Selena croaked between stiff lips, not exactly sure she did understand. She had seen nothing of Max, herself, before they had left, but she was aware he must have talked to Pearl.

'I mean you—you can get out of here!' Pearl raged, her face so hard with anger she looked quite ugly. 'You little fool!' she spat. 'You could have had him eating out of your hand, but you didn't even try. Did you have to turn down everything he suggested? You wouldn't even agree to the simplest thing for my sake! After all I've done for you, you didn't think twice about ruining my career.'

'How can it be ruined?' Selena gasped.

'How can it not be?' Pearl retorted bitterly. 'Everyone who matters is going to know that Max turned me down. No one's going to offer me anything decent after this. Well,' as Selena stared at her numbly, 'I'm off to Bermuda with Dickie French and you can go to hell for all I care, but you aren't staying here!'

'I'll—I'll find somewhere.'

'You'd better—and at once!' Pearl snarled. 'Why don't you try Mummy and that sweet step-daddy of yours, who seems to fancy you quite a lot?'

'You're crazy!' Selena whispered incredulously.

'Am I?' Pearl blazed, 'I don't think so! What do you think they fought about so much when they were last over? He couldn't keep his eyes off you, and she knew it.'

'You're imagining things! And Mother does have a name.' Selena tried to speak steadily, but her voice trembled and she felt sick again. As sick as she had felt all morning.

'I'm not going to argue about it.' Pearl's eyes were still diamond-hard. 'Just get packed and get out, so I can leave knowing you're gone. If you don't I'll throw you out myself!'

Half an hour later Selena sat on a seat in Regent's Park, blindly watching the wind playing little games on the boating lake. White-faced and stunned, she wondered what more could happen to her today, what she could do. Fleetingly, when Pearl had first ordered her out, she had thought of her mother, but Pearl's subsequent remarks ruled out such a possibility. Small incidents regarding Chris, her stepfather, came back to Selena, which hadn't really registered at the time. Perhaps Pearl was exaggerating, she had a vile tongue when she lost her temper, but she had succeeded in making Selena uneasy. Too uneasy, somehow, to risk seeking refuge with her mother and upsetting her new marriage.

She had thought of asking Ronald if he could suggest anything, but when she rang his housekeeper told her he had been unexpectedly called away. He might not be home until the end of the month, or probably the next. Which appeared to rule out any hope of help in that direction.

Despondently Selena sat on in the Park and considered. She did have some money, but she wasn't sure where she could stay. There were plenty of decent places, but she wasn't sure whether she could afford to stay in any one of them for long. She certainly wouldn't be able to look for anything permanent until she was earning more money.

Somewhere decent? The words revolved around her tired mind for quite a while before suggesting anything. Then suddenly it occurred to her. Why not visit her house in Devon? The solicitor, whom she had been in touch with, had implied, if only by his manner that it was scarcely worth visiting, but it might be no worse than the best she could afford in London. She had her sleeping bag and if the bedrooms weren't habitable she could always sleep in the kitchen. Having been left the house, she would have to take a look at it one day, anyway, and it could be one way of solving her immediate problems?

She sat a little longer, forcing herself to think it over sensibly, bitterly reflecting how she had been too easily persuaded to act rashly in the past. She was grateful, though, for anything which might take her thoughts away from Max. Perhaps Pearl, in turning her out, had been kinder than she had realised.

Having at last made up her mind, Selena considered the unhappy state of her bank balance. In all, she would have less than a hundred pounds, and this only because of a small cheque her father had belatedly sent for her birthday and some overdue wages Ronald had paid her. Out of this she owed Pearl twenty pounds for board and lodgings, a sum which she usually paid over each Friday evening. This Friday they had both been too excited and worried over Max's invitation to remember. This didn't mean, of course, that such a debt could be written off. If she took a temporary loan of it to help tide her over, Selena vowed she would send Pearl the money just as soon as she returned from Bermuda.

Here Selena paused in her thinking, drawing a trembling breath. She still had Max's money, almost burning a hole in her tortured mind. This she had intended, at Lynton, to return to him personally, having an almost demented determination to make sure he received it. After dressing, she had quickly packed her case before rushing downstairs to enquire where he was. She had been unable to find him. There had only been Pearl, waiting in the hall, and she had been informed that Max had already left. Too late, Selena had realised her opportunity had gone. Before she quite understood what was happening, she and Pearl had been escorted to a waiting taxi, and she had found it impossible to hand over a bundle of unwrapped notes to the very superior-looking butler, without any sort of explanation, especially in front of Pearl.

As she had no address to send it to, like the money she owed Pearl, she decided she must keep it for the time being, and she sealed it away in the bottom of her bag. She would never touch a penny of it, but it might serve to remind her of how easily an unwary girl might ruin her whole life. How easy it was, she thought bitterly, to fall in love with a man without scruples, when one didn't stop to think.

Although she did now try to think sensibly, Selena was aware that most decisions taken hastily had to be acted on swiftly, or they would never come to anything. So she didn't pause to examine all the pitfalls attached to going to Devon until she was actually sitting on the train. She wasn't sure that she would be able to reach her destination before dark, but it could be less expensive to stay in Exeter than in London. And she would rather be out of London as it reminded her too vividly of Max.

Every time she thought of him she felt tense and ill, and she was relieved she had the carriage almost to herself. There was no one to see the white strain on her face or notice the occasional painful tear running down her cheek. Bitterly she wondered how Max could have treated her as he had done, then dared to walk away as if nothing had happened. Worse still to have left a note, in which he had made it quite clear he considered her a cheap little nobody who could be disposed of with a handful of cash.

She wasn't naïve enough to believe that a relationship between a man and a woman could stand still, nor was she so simple as to imagine there could have been anything permanent between herself and a man like Max Heger. Knowing this, she couldn't believe she had ever given him reason to act as he had done. Hadn't she always been the one to hold back?

Or had she? The hatred in her heart, warring with her innate honesty, brought a frown of painful indecision to her face. She had returned his kisses—more than that, she had clung to him, put her arms around him, in such a way as might have given him the impression that she was begging to be held closer. Yet she was sure she had never deliberately set out to lead him on. Always, when he kissed her, she hadn't seemed able to help herself, and she had responded with a passion which had been impossible to hide from him. She might have tried to, but with his experience he must have guessed.

She hadn't realised she was capable of such response; certainly it was something she had never experienced with another man. But Max hadn't known this and had immediately jumped to the wrong conclusions, especially after misconstruing her telephone call to Ronald. He must have thought she had intended starting an affair with Ronald, when she had merely been discussing work. It must have been this conviction which had encouraged him to take her to bed and make love to her.

All the same, she would never forgive him. Not that it was likely she would be given the chance. She didn't suppose she would ever see him again. Now she felt besmirched and used, ruined for any other man. Now she must reorganise her whole life, putting out of her head for ever all thought of marriage. Perhaps, she thought wearily, during the next few weeks, in the quiet of the Devonshire countryside, she might learn to live with herself again and be able to decide the best way to do it.

As it was almost dark in Exeter when she arrived she decided to stay overnight and set out in the morning to try and find her house. The solicitor had said there would be someone to let her in, which, thinking about it now, seemed rather strange. Had he meant the door wouldn't be locked, or, which was perhaps more likely, that he had left the key with an obliging neighbour?

Next morning Selena caught a bus travelling southwest, past towns with the intriguing names of Chudleigh, Ashburton and Buckfastleigh. The journey wasn't too long in actual miles but proved complicated towards the end as she wasn't sure of her property's exact location, and no one appeared to have even heard of it. As she drew nearer her destination, the countryside grew wilder and the villages smaller, with the distances between them longer. Long before she arrived at the one she sought, Selena was convinced she was lost. In the last village, however, when she stopped outside a picturesque thatched cottage, to ask without much hope for directions, the elderly lady whom she spoke to was able to tell her precisely where her house was.

'About a mile farther on from where the bus put you down, then just a few yards up a track. I believe you can see the house from the road.'

Selena thanked her gratefully and went on, carefully memorising the instructions. The mile she judged to be approximately right, but the few yards of track wasn't. True, she could see the top of the house from the road, but the track itself must have been nearly another mile long. But it was the condition of this, more than its length, that filled her with dismay. It was so deeply rutted that, even if the house was saleable, the state of its drive might be enough to put any prospective buyer off.

When she first saw the house she feared she must have come to the wrong place after all, as smoke was curling out of the chimney. This house was apparently occupied. Believing this, she spared it no more than a brief glance and was surprised when the woman who came to the door told her she hadn't made a mistake. When Selena, rather taken aback, said she hadn't expected to find anyone here, the woman replied that she had lived with the late owner, Selena's mother's cousin, all her life, first as maid and then as housekeeper, and when the old lady died, the solicitor had asked her to stay on and keep an eye on the place until the new owner arrived.

'My name is Bronwen,' she said, 'because my mother was Welsh. I'm seventy years old and I thought I'd done with surprises, but I never dreamt the new owner would be a young lady like you.'

As Selena followed her into an old-fashioned parlour, she found herself confessing frankly, 'I don't really know how I came to be the new owner. Miss Hartley never saw me, she didn't know me, yet she left me her house. I—I believe she didn't approve of my mother being divorced?'

'No, she wouldn't,' Bronwen said dryly, standing, hands folded over her spotless white apron, surveying Selena keenly.

Selena stared around the shabby but cosy little room curiously. 'It's a wonder she didn't leave it to you.'

'Oh, she wouldn't do that, dearie!' Bronwen looked shocked. 'She had a proper belief in the rightness of things, and I was only her servant.'

'After all those years!'

'Made no difference to her, it didn't,' Bronwen nodded her neat grey head in approval. 'I won't hear a word against her, mind you. She was very good to me, always treat me like a friend, but we both knew our places.'

Which should have explained everything, Selena supposed, feeling not a great deal wiser.

Bronwen went on to explain proudly that there were two small rooms down and two up, and a kitchen over which she slept, snug and warm. 'And there's a nice cottage I can have in the village whenever you're finished with me,' she said.

Selena felt that, as Bronwen and she had just met, things were moving too fast, but she recognised that Bronwen, although a calm-looking woman, was very anxious about the future. For weeks she had probably had it on her mind and now there were questions she could contain no longer.

Reluctantly Selena tried to explain that she had no money to pay wages. 'Unless I can get a job I shan't even have enough to run the house,' she confessed.

Bronwen glanced at her sharply, frowning at the girl's drawn young face and thin body. 'You don't look strong enough to manage either a job or a house,' she said bluntly. 'I'd have thought you were on the point of collapse.'

'Of course I'm not,' Selena said, and immediately slid unconsciousness to the floor.

The doctor, called by Bronwen, after she had failed to revive Selena, was very sure of his diagnosis. When Selena came to, he was bending over her.

'Physically you're in quite good shape, young lady, but you're far too thin, and I believe you've had some kind of shock. In fact I'm sure of it.'

He talked some more and she admitted guardedly that she had, but refused to tell him anything else.

'I'll leave you a sedative,' he said before he went. 'I'll look in again tomorrow.'

Bronwen fussed. 'I'll look after you now,' she said.

Anxiously Selena stared up at her, from where she lay on the old-fashioned sofa. 'But I can't pay you!'

'Who's said anything about payment, my pretty maid? I have my pension and a roof over my head.'

Surely that wasn't enough, Selena worried, yet she was dismayed to find she was too weak to argue. Both her body and spirits felt so crushed she couldn't find the energy to protest further.

For the rest of the day she was sick and her head ached almost as badly as her heart, but next morning she felt surprisingly better. For breakfast she could only manage a cup of tea and half a piece of toast, but she felt well enough to have a proper look around, and to talk seriously to Bronwen.

The house was in fairly good order. It just needed decorating and odd repairs. The outbuildings were not so good, but if they could be tidied up and given a coat of whitewash or something, they might look presentable. These, along with the house and the five acres of land which went with it, might attract the attention of some enterprising family who wanted to get away from it all and become self-supporting. People who might be hardy enough to ignore the unconcealable disadvantages. Despondently Selena wandered around. What she really needed was a man to help her. A bitter twist came to her lips as she thought of one in particular.

Bronwen agreed generally with her conclusions that the place had possibilities.

They were having coffee in the kitchen while discussing the matter thoroughly, which Selena knew was the only way. 'I'll have to get work,' she said, 'in order to pay for material to carry out the necessary repairs and the painting.' Wistfully she thought of Max's money, lying idly at the bottom of her bag, but closed her mind firmly against such temptation.

'Even if you could find work, you wouldn't be able to travel daily from here,' Bronwen warned her.

'What about the village?' Selena asked hopefully.

'There's never anything there,' Bronwen began, then paused. 'Well, I have heard that the doctor's receptionist is leaving soon, but you would have to have the right qualifications, wouldn't you?'

'I can type and keep books,' Selena told her.

'You'd better be asking the doctor, then, when he calls.' As Selena nodded, her face considerably brighter, Bronwen informed her gruffly that she had some savings of her own. 'The money's only lying in the bank doing nothing,' she said. 'I could let you have what you want and you could repay me after you sell the house.'

'If I can find a buyer,' Selena warned, but she was touched by such open generosity and could see that Bronwen might be hurt if she turned her offer down. 'I tell you what,' she smiled warmly, 'I'll accept a loan gladly, but only on condition that you take it back with proper interest, after the house is sold. I'm also going to insist that you take something for looking after Moor Edge since my cousin died, as well as for the weeks you work for me.'

'Well, I can't lose, can I, but you'd better make sure there's going to be something left for yourself.' Bronwen returned Selena's smile wryly, but with a surprising tear in her eye.

The doctor was surprised to learn Selena was looking for work, but agreed to take her on after the girl he had now left to be married in two weeks' time. Selena would need a little while to recover, he said, without being more specific.

Fearing he suspected something of what was wrong with her, Selena went cold with misery after she had seen him out. Didn't he realise that hard work and lots of it was the only answer to her kind of problem?

Yet for all her impatience, she found she had to wait several days before she was able to do very much, and then she still felt terrible. The shock and bitterness following her last night with Max Heger seemed to have drained her completely. Eventually, however, she forced herself to make a start. After a local paint shop had agreed to deliver whatever decorating material she ordered, Selena decided to begin on the outbuildings.

Since she was so filled with determination, it vexed her when she made little progress. Bronwen sighed over her impatience and said she shouldn't be in such a hurry, but Selena found it difficult to relax. Whitewashing was such a routine job it left her with too much time to think, and no matter how hard she worked, at night she was unable to sleep.

Upstairs she used the largest of the two small bedrooms, and here she tried to get through the long dark hours of each night by reading some of the old classics she found downstairs. Some of them she had read at school and it was like meeting old friends, but tonight, although she tried desperately hard, she couldn't concentrate.

It was after midnight. Sighing, she laid her book aside, but left the light on, because the darkness brought nightmares of Max. Last night she had dreamt she was in his arms and he was kissing her, crushing her against him, under him, until she had been consumed by a wild, terrible pain she couldn't escape. When she woke with a start, it had been to find herself wet with sweat and gasping, her hands clenched into tight little fists pushing someone away who wasn't there.

Full of continuing anguish, as she remembered, she turned on her face, but now her clenched hands beat despairingly against the top of her wooden bed. When, moments later, she stopped, exhausted, the knocking went on.

Thinking her ears were playing tricks on her overwrought imagination, Selena went tense, then suddenly she sat up. Someone was knocking, she could hear them downstairs, on the front door. Slowly she got out of bed and walked quietly across the room. Her window overlooked the front door and she carefully pressed her face against the glass. It was a wild night, dark with a high wind blowing, driving rain in floods against the house, but she could just make out the tall figure of a man standing below. He appeared to be swaying, unless it was the wind that gave this impression, as he reached again for the knocker.

Nervously Selena started back, fright chilling her very bones. Who could he be, what could he want? Why would a man be knocking on their door at this time of night? Could she ignore the knocking and hope he would go away? Perhaps, she frowned, he might be injured, in need of help. How could she ignore him? If he was injured and wandered off again over the moors, he could be found dead in the morning.

Swiftly, knowing she could stand arguing with herself for hours as to the sensible thing to do, she switched on the light she had extinguished before getting out of bed and reached for her dressing-gown. Bronwen was deaf and would sleep soundly through any amount of knocking, especially on a night like this.

Without pausing to wonder again if she was being foolhardy, Selena unlocked the front door and opened it. It was as if something stronger than herself compelled her to. To her astonished apprehension, the man with his hand still on the knocker almost fell on top of her. With a sharp cry she raised protective hands to push him off, and immediately she touched him she felt a burning sensation. But when she raised startled eyes to his face she almost fainted. The man, tall and dark, who had staggered drunkenly into the small hall was none other but Max Heger!

She was unable to believe it. At first she thought it must be because of her bad dreams, until, staring at him in wild-eyed horror, she realised she wasn't mistaken. As he struggled beside her, as though trying to regain his balance, she opened her mouth to gasp his name, but no sound came. Her throat was locked so tight she couldn't speak. Then, to her further amazement, she saw there was no recognition in the eyes he turned on her. They were dark and quite blank in the white, blood-streaked haggardness of his face.

'I'm sorry, Mrs—Miss . . .' he apologised thickly, 'I'm

sorry to bother you like this, but I don't seem to know where I am.'

Continuing to stare at him with incredulous eyes, Selena took another minute to find her voice. 'It's a place called Moor Edge,' she whispered. 'Only a house, it's probably not even on the map.'

'Not on the map,' he repeated, putting a shaking hand to his head. His eyes were dull, dark with frustration. 'To tell you the truth,' he said savagely, 'I have no idea where I am, or what the hell I'm doing here!'

Selena's breath had gone again. Her heart was hammering, her stomach churning, making her feel sick. She would have pushed him back, out of the door if her legs hadn't felt so weak. How dared he come here, shattering her hard-won equilibrium? It hadn't amounted to much, and now it was gone, leaving her almost instantly as shaken and as vulnerable as she had been the last time she had seen him. What sort of game was he playing? Why did he pretend not to recognise her? If he was pretending! As she knew her first stirrings of doubt, she caught sight of the blood caked on his head. It was obvious he had suffered some kind of blow that might have affected his memory. Uncertainly she hesitated, holding back the bitter tirade fighting to escape her taut lips.

'Have you been involved in an accident?' she forced herself to ask evenly.

'I don't know, I'm telling you!' he put his hand to his head again with a grim groan, as he jerked it away and saw the blood on it. 'I guess I must have been,' he muttered, his glance shifting over Selena's pale face as if trying to focus. 'I only know I was lying on the side of the road, and I picked myself up and came here. I saw a light.'

Her reading lamp, shining through her bedroom window, visible from the road. He must have followed it down the length of the track to the house. Yet still she felt unable to trust what her intuition told her was the truth. Suspicion clouded her darkened eyes as she exclaimed. 'You can't have been wandering about Dartmoor at this time of year without a coat.' He only wore a shirt and pants. 'Have you a car?'

'How the hell would I know?' he snapped savagely, then as he saw her shrink, he apologised, 'I'm sorry. It was good of you to let me in and all I seem able to do is shout at you!' His mouth twisted. 'You can't know what it feels like not to know who you are.'

He had a lot of mud on his trousers, not so much on his shirt. It was his head that seemed to have come off worst. It looked as if he had been walking and knocked down by some hit-and-run driver? Perhaps he had left his coat in his car while he got out to look for something.

'Do you think I could sit down for a minute?' he asked suddenly, more humbly. 'I feel terrible.'

'If you like.' Swallowing hard, Selena led him through the small dining-room into the warm kitchen. Putting him into a chair, she watched wide-eyed as he slumped against the table and closed his eyes. Even to touch him briefly had unnerved her, making her feel dreadful.

With difficulty she controlled her trembling limbs. She could do nothing about her heart, which was going twice as fast as usual, but she did manage to stop shaking. Max had his eyes heavily shut and looked really ill.

Bronwen, although deaf, had instincts trained by a lifetime spent on the moors. Something had woken her, and she knew something was wrong. 'What is it?' she asked, stumbling down the back stairs into the kitchen, her old eyes travelling shrewdly over Max's tall, well-made figure. 'This man's been hurt. Who is he?'

Selena thought she had done with impulsive decisions, but suddenly she decided not to confess she knew who Max was. He could have a double, she excused herself. Glancing at Bronwen, she shrugged. 'He was knocking at the door, and appears to have hurt his head. He insists that he can't remember who he is, or what he's doing here.'

'Where's his coat?' Bronwen moved nearer Max, whose head still lay in his arms, his eyes still closed.

'He wasn't wearing one.'

'A hit-and-run driver, I should think.' Bronwen confirmed Selena's suspicions as she ran an experienced hand over Max's brow. 'He certainly has a beautiful bump. Have you felt it?'

'No!' Selena drew back as though stung.

Fortunately Bronwen was too busy concentrating on Max to notice how white she had gone. 'Whoever did it probably took his coat, with his wallet in it. You're lucky if they leave your shirt, these days,' she glanced keenly at Selena. 'You did say you don't know him?'

'No, I don't know him.' Doing her best to avoid Bronwen's probing glance, Selena turned to look at Max hollowly. 'But I should think he needs help.'

'Yes,' Bronwen nodded, 'no question of that. We'll have to get the doctor out again in the morning.'

'In the morning?' Selena was icy cold with dislike as she stared at Max, but she was also filled with a terrible consuming anxiety. She couldn't account for it, but it was there, threatening to tear her to pieces. 'The morning could be too late, Bronwen. I'll go now.'

'It's the middle of the night, Miss Selena, and you aren't well yourself,' Bronwen protested.

'I still think the morning might be too late,' Selena insisted stubbornly. Then, as another thought struck her, 'Are you nervous of staying here alone with him?'

Bronwen shook her head. 'Not in his condition. I would say he's strong enough normally, but right now I think it would take him all his time to stand up. No, dearie, it's you I'm worrying about, not this gentleman.'

Gentleman! Selena could have laughed aloud as she ignored Bronwen's pleas about the state of the road and the weather and reached for her coat. If Bronwen only knew! As she let herself out of the house, Selena didn't pause to wonder why she should be so willing to risk getting soaked and lost on a night like this. If she did occasionally reflect, she kept telling herself it was something she would have done for anyone.

The doctor had just come in from delivering a baby and, after a caustic comment on her bedraggled state, he took her straight back to Moor Edge.

'We do get strangers lost on the moors,' he said, 'but always try to make sure they're really in need of urgent attention before risking your own life.'

She waited, hands clenched, nails digging into her skin, while he examined Max briefly. 'Curious,' he muttered, 'he doesn't look the type to be wandering around in his shirt sleeves, but you never can tell..Some of the most unlikely people seem to be finding life too much for them and taking to the road. I wonder who he is.'

Bronwen said nothing, neither did Selena.

'However,' the doctor went on, 'there could be a very simple explanation. We'd better wait until daylight before we jump to any more conclusions.'

'Meanwhile, what's to be done with him, doctor?' asked Bronwen.

'He'll have to stay here, of course!' Selena exclaimed, then flushed. Why had she said that when she couldn't bear even to look at Max any more? 'I mean,' she stammered weakly, aware that both Bronwen and the doctor were staring at her oddly, 'we couldn't turn him out in the state he's in! Could we?'

'I'd better run him to hospital,' Dr Lewis replied. 'We could get an ambulance, but that would take longer than it would take me to do the job myself. And an ambulance could easily break an axle on that track of yours in the dark. I know what to look for, having had to attend Miss Hartley.'

'Hospital?' Selena frowned as Bronwen nodded her head.

'Best place to make sure there's no permanent damage.' Dr Lewis was already preparing his patient. 'He should be X-rayed, to make sure there's nothing more than simple amnesia. Then we'll see.'

Max, still dazed and ill, made little attempt to argue. 'I'll go anywhere,' he groaned, 'if it will help me recover my memory.'

'It might return very quickly, but the most important thing at the moment is to get you to hospital,' the doctor reassured him, before turning with a frown to Selena.

'I think I'll have to ask you to come with us, my dear. He's going to need someone to sit beside him and hold him while I negotiate the holes in the road out there. Whatever damage has been done to this man's head, I shouldn't like to be responsible for making it worse.'

CHAPTER SEVEN

HAVING agreed readily enough to do what the doctor asked, Selena wasn't prepared for the way in which Max sagged against her every time the car lurched to avoid a hole in the track. Drawing a deep breath, she forced herself to endure it without crying out.

Why had Max come here? While seeking the doctor, an hour ago, she had been so busy struggling against the elements she hadn't had much chance to ask herself. Now she wondered about it apprehensively. She was aware that the location for his next film was Devon, but she had understood that only a small part of it was to be made there, and they weren't due to begin properly for at least another two months. Obviously Max's plans must have changed, but his coming here could have nothing to do with her. He couldn't have had any idea where she was as Pearl was away, and even if Pearl hadn't been she wouldn't have been able to tell him, if he had asked.

More convinced than ever that his arrival here had nothing to do with herself, Selena decided he had simply been trying to get the feel of the countryside. She knew little about making films, but he had once told her this was important. Perhaps he had been searching for one particular spot, and when he found it intending to linger for a while, possibly making last-minute alterations to the script. He was a fanatic, Pearl had said, for getting things exactly right. It must merely have been one of those odd twists of fate which had caused him to be knocked down where he had been, then to have seen the light in her room. If it hadn't been for her light he might have walked on and she would never have known.

Staring at him now, in the darkness of the doctor's

car, she felt hot inside but cold out. Her pulse racing, she tried to remember how she had felt when he had made love to her. It was a question she had tried to ignore since it had happened. She had considered other aspects of their relationship, but never that. How had she reacted in the final outcome? She could only recall spinning, caught up in a mounting passion, like a tide running strongly. There had been the molten, sensual heat of it, the touch of his mouth like a flame on her naked skin, but that had been the last thing she was conscious of. It had been too much, which must be why she had passed out. Mercifully, perhaps, as to be fully aware of what had happened next could only have added to her shame.

When Max's head slumped again on to her shoulder and she had to put both arms around him this time to prevent him from falling, the almost dead weight of his half unconscious body was more than she could bear. It took a terrible effort not to push him away, to stop herself from hitting him, from trying to hurt him and make him suffer as much as she had done.

At the hospital Dr Lewis advised her to stay in the car until he returned. Nodding her assent, she watched numbly as stretcher-bearers bore Max away. The doctor apologised half an hour later for keeping her waiting. He had wanted to see Max comfortably settled, he said.

As he turned the car and headed for home, he smiled wryly. 'You might be interested to know that two of the nurses have christened him Nero, until he remembers his own name. It's Latin and means dark-complexioned, black-haired.'

As he dropped her off, he said, 'I'll let you know tomorrow how he's progressing, unless you care to ring the hospital yourself.'

It was easy, Selena kept telling herself, not to make enquiries about a man you despised, but the next three days were the longest she could ever remember living through. Desperately she tried to lose herself in work.

There was plenty to do, but worry over Max made her far more tired and irritable than the amount of work she got through.

Bronwen didn't know this, of course. 'What we need here is a man,' she sighed, little dreaming that they were about to get one.

On the morning of the third day, Dr Lewis called to tell them that Max was ready to leave hospital and would like to come and stay with them.

'Has his memory returned yet?' Bronwen asked doubtfully, while Selena was stunned to silence.

'No. Otherwise I don't think he would have made such a request,' Dr Lewis said frankly. 'I have no means of knowing what his background is, but I feel it won't be a lonely old house on the moors.'

'What about the police?' Bronwen glanced hard at Selena, clearly puzzled as to why she didn't speak.

'They've been informed,' the doctor assured her, 'but they can't help much. They've had no enquiries about anyone like him.'

'Have they found his car?' Bronwen asked.

'No,' again the doctor shook his head, 'no car has been found or any trace of one, so it looks as if our friend didn't have one. The police have found the place where it appears he was knocked down. There are tyre marks but no sign of any great struggle. They believe he must have been knocked unconscious and whoever did it made off with his money and any form of identity.'

Bronwen muttered anxiously, 'I suppose the police will do their best.'

'We've got to remember,' Dr Lewis said, 'that there might be no one looking for him, or that he may not want to be found. Until he's proved guilty of something he has all the rights of a private citizen.'

Feeling cold with guilt yet driven by an unyielding reluctance to reveal Max's identity, Selena spoke at last. 'Is he really well enough to leave hospital?'

'Yes,' the doctor replied, 'but he has nowhere to go

and no money. He's recovered fairly well, but I should like to be able to keep an eye on him until he recovers his memory.'

'How long will that take?' Bronwen enquired quickly.

'It's difficult to say. It could be a week—a year. At the moment he's half mad with frustration.'

'I'm not sure. I don't know if it would be wise.' Bronwen talked as though the decision was hers, but Selena interrupted her, something driving her almost against her will.

'We could let him stay a few days, Bronwen. We can always see how we get on.'

'Couldn't you have him?' Bronwen, clearly uneasy, turned to the doctor sharply.

'I would have offered,' he said, 'but I'm not married and, as I expect you're fully aware,' he continued dryly, 'my domestic life is difficult enough as it is. However, I don't think he's ready to face my kind of household yet, and it's the quiet here that seems to attract him. Amnesia, you know, can make even the strongest men nervous.'

Bronwen pursed her lips, saying nothing more, leaving the final outcome to Selena.

'Mind you,' the doctor added, 'I'm not altogether sure I approve, but I did promise him I'd ask you. If you'd visited him in hospital, Selena, I'm sure he would have asked you himself. I'm merely passing on a message.'

The doctor's eyes, as he watched Selena, were curious and she knew he was wondering why, when she had run all the way to the village for help for him, she had subsequently ignored the strangers existence.

Again she let the chance of confessing slip by, and in the confusion of the moment found herself nodding her head and saying she had been busy, but of course Max could come if it would help. Only she didn't call him Max, she called him Nero, with what she hoped was a natural-looking smile.

When Max arrived later in the day with the doctor,

he was so changed she almost gasped. He looked the same, apart from being paler; it was his manner which was different. Always before he had been decisively cool and confident, very sure of himself. The man who followed Dr Lewis into the house that afternoon was far from confident. His eyes were uncertain, his expression slightly hunted as he gazed around, as if he desperately sought something which might jerk him back to total reality. When he saw Selena he seemed filled by such humble gratitude she wanted to cry out in protest, but there was no spark of recognition in the close gaze he fixed on her.

Some of the tension going out of her, Selena released a nervous breath. She felt better, but only for a moment. As she remembered what he was, what he had done to her, her heart returned to its frozen hardness. She wasn't sure yet what his motives had been in visiting this particular part of the country, nor was she sure of her own, in allowing him to come here, but unashamedly she knew it had something to do with revenge. She hadn't worked it out yet, but she firmly believed that the next few days or weeks would provide the only opportunity for revenge she was likely to get, and if she let such a chance pass it would never come again.

After the doctor had gone, while Bronwen cleared the tea things, Selena took Max upstairs and showed him his room. It was next to hers, the only spare room they had, and it was small. Selena doubted if he would find much comfort in the narrow single bed, but she had dismissed Bronwen's suggestion that they should bring a larger one out of the attic.

'If he's only staying for a short time it wouldn't be worth it,' she said.

'His feet will stick out the bottom of this one,' Bronwen had replied, with obvious disapproval.

Which Selena had ignored as she proceeded to make up the bed with the roughest linen sheets she could find. 'Those belonged to Miss Hartley's mother.'

Bronwen's frown had deepened. 'They've never been used. They should be properly washed and boiled first.'

'If he's been tramping the roads he'll be used to something rougher than this,' Selena had finished the bed and given it a coldly satisfied pat as she thought of Max spending restless nights in it. He might have supplied her with more comfortable accommodation, but only with the intention of seducing her.

To her chagrin, as she stood aside to show him the small bare room, he seemed pleased with it, his face full of humble appreciation. She wasn't sure if this was what she was looking for. He wouldn't suffer for his sins if he was filled with overwhelming gratitude for everything she did.

It wasn't until after dinner, which he ate hungrily if with a peculiar reluctance, that she thought she had found the answer. Max had been very quiet, scarcely saying a word throughout the meal. Now, as if able to remember the doctor telling him Selena was the owner of Moor Edge, he asked if he could speak to her privately.

About to retort that whatever he had to say must be said in front of Bronwen, Selena hesitated. Her heart fluttered with alarm. Just supposing he had remembered something? It would never do for Bronwen to hear of it.

Her eyes colder than she realised, she led the way to the sitting room. Her heart was racing again, she could feel it, but apart from this she had herself well under control.

She didn't ask him to sit down, and while the man she had known might have taken a chair automatically, the new, more hesitant Max Heger remained standing. Selena's eyes remained cold as she seated herself in one of the two comfortable armchairs and stared at him. It was gratifying how her deep-rooted anger enabled her to do this. She might still love him in a way, but this emotion could now be entirely subdued by the force of her determination for revenge.

Slowly, feeling rather like the actress he had asked her to be, she looked up from her apparent absorption with the glowing fire. Meeting the anxious uncertainty in his eyes, she almost laughed aloud. Max was despondent, unsure of himself, his pride in the dust. He even looked as though he might be shaking under the tight control he was keeping on himself.

'Yes?' she prompted, allowing her own eyes to display only a fine hauteur.

He spoke at last, obviously finding it difficult. 'I wanted to apologise for the trouble I've caused you in coming here. I'll try not to be a nuisance.'

He sounded so abject she winced. The new Max took some getting used to. 'I shouldn't worry too much about it,' she spoke so calmly she almost startled herself. 'You had to go somewhere, and we can always put up with you for a few days.'

It was Max's turn to wince, although he appeared to find nothing unreasonable about her tone or comments. 'I also wanted to say,' he muttered, 'that I'll compensate you for all your trouble, once my memory returns.'

That he should mention compensation was all Selena needed to make her smouldering anger flare. The beast! The vile scoundrel! Did he believe she was willing to do anything for money? With a disdain which clearly bewildered him she said tightly, with the deliberate intention of making him grovel, 'I should make sure you have some money first, before you make any rash promises.'

Colour ran dark red under his skin. 'I deserved that, I suppose. No, I quite agree. I may be a pauper, and it's not a risk I should be asking you to take.'

'But you are asking, aren't you?'

'Yes.' His colour ebbed again, leaving him grey and haggard. 'Have I any other option?'

His bitter frustration was good to hear. 'No,' she replied tartly. For the present it suited her that he should believe this.

'I'm praying it won't be for long.' Almost pleadingly he stared at her, his eyes tormented. 'You can't know what it's like to face blank walls whichever way you turn. Surely someone should know who I am?'

'What makes you think anyone should?' she taunted. 'You're most likely a drop-out. Perhaps you don't have a family or anyone who wants to know you?'

'Of course, you're right.' To her amazement he accepted her mocking comments without a murmur, his broad shoulders slumped as he ran a hopeless hand through his thick black hair.

She might have felt sorry for him if she hadn't hated him so much, but if he was suffering it was no more than he deserved. A man who had acted as he had done deserved to be punished!

The fierceness of her voice reflecting her contempt, she exclaimed. 'Now, if you're quite finished, I suggest you stop feeling sorry for yourself and go back to the kitchen. As soon as you feel well enough,' she added sarcastically, 'I promise I'll find you plenty of work to do, so when you do recover your memory and discover you have no money, I shan't be on your conscience!'

Why hadn't she thought of that before? After Max had obediently departed, Selena felt stunned by the brilliance of her own inspiration. She would get Max to clean up the buildings—the whole property. Hadn't Bronwen said they needed a man? Well, now they had one, and she would make him work like a slave! Dr Lewis had said Max was quite fit physically, and wouldn't she enjoy seeing his face when his memory returned and he discovered the kind of work he had been doing? Quickly she turned her mind from the opinion he might express of her that day. Long before then she hoped to have extracted more than her share of retribution!

Ever since the morning Max had come knocking on her door, Selena had listened to every news bulletin.

Knowing he was a man of some importance, both here and abroad, she felt sure he would eventually be reported as missing, but as the days went by and there was no mention of him she could only conclude that he had left the States for reasons of his own and no one, as yet, suspected he was missing.

The morning after he arrived from hospital, she was surprised to find him already in the kitchen when she came down to breakfast.

'You're up early?' she said coolly.

'You said something about work,' he replied quietly, accepting the plate of bacon and eggs Bronwen passed him, with a grateful if slightly worried word of thanks.

'Your memory is good enough at times,' Selena dared sharply.

Although he glanced at her quickly, he didn't take offence. 'Yes,' he admitted, 'I quite agree. I can remember everything they did for me in hospital, but nothing of what happened before I came here.'

'What a shame!' Selena curled her lips deliberately. 'Or could it be a blessing in disguise?'

Max didn't appear offended by this, either, but he did lay down his knife and fork as if his appetite had gone. 'How could it be?' he asked heavily.

The small twinge of shame she felt didn't stop her, not even Bronwen's surprised disapproval did that. 'You could be a criminal for all we know!' she burst out.

'The police don't think so,' he said, but his eyes darkened anxiously.

'You could have murdered your wife and left her with a dozen kids to bring up!'

'Miss Selena!' Bronwen gasped, quite shocked.

Selena, quickly seeing her mistake, said she was sorry. She wasn't, and she was conscious that Max was aware of it too. For all his mental confusion he didn't mistake her spite for mounting panic, as Bronwen charitably did. Yet that served as a warning. On no account must Bronwen suspect what she was up to. In future she mus keep her verbal taunts for when Max and she were alone.

She wished he wouldn't stare at her so hard. During the whole of breakfast his eyes scarcely seemed to leave her face.

'Do you feel up to working this morning?' she asked at last. He looked far from well, his face strained, his eyes sunken, as if he hadn't slept much. This, she decided, was probably the fault of his bed more than anything else. She tried to imagine his tall body and broad shoulders fitting into it and failed. Instead she concentrated bitterly on what he had done to her, succeeding so well that when he said he would enjoy doing something, she didn't argue.

'You'd better come with me, then,' she shrugged.

Bronwen, although she shook her head, produced a pair of overalls which an odd job man had once left. Max, appreciating her gesture, said he would get some of his own as soon as he got the chance, but as he caught Selena's mocking glance he flushed.

Realising there was a lot she could convey without words, Selena took him to one of the large barns, where they worked steadily throughout the rest of the day with only a short break for lunch. At five, by which time Max was beginning to look really ill, she decided to stop. She felt tired herself, and it wouldn't be sensible to kill Max off at the first opportunity, not even if she felt like it.

'Come along, Nero,' she spoke scornfully, as if he were a dog she despised. 'You aren't very strong for so big a man, are you? We'd better call it a day.'

Bleakly his eyes darkened. 'I'll improve in a day or two, I expect.'

'How do you like your new name?' she asked.

'Nero?' He lifted his dark brows indifferently. 'I suppose it's as good as any until I learn what my real name is.'

'You'd better have a bath,' she suggested abruptly,

preferring not to believe that day would arrive.

He was coming out of the bathroom as she went to go in. Someone at the hospital must have found him a short robe, two sizes too small. It was stretched with an embarrasing tightness around his well made figure, and she quickly averted her eyes. He needed a shave, she noticed, heat stinging her cold cheeks, but she certainly wasn't going to supply a razor!

'You took your time, didn't you?' she snapped at him. 'You might remember, in future, that we've only one bathroom.'

Colour crept painfully over his tanned skin. His strong mouth tightened, but only fleetingly. Again a hunted expression took over, the anger which he might normally have shown at her tone fading. 'I'm sorry,' he muttered, staring at her.

What was there about her to make him stare so consistently? At odd times during the day she had felt the intentness of his gaze. It made her uneasy. It was as if something behind his amnesia was struggling to enlighten him about her. Well, she told herself, what did it matter if he did remember? Whatever she was doing, hadn't he driven her to it, and nothing she could do would ever be as bad as his initial crime. With a cool inclination of her head she swept past him into the bathroom.

During the next few days they continued working together on the buildings. As Max's strength returned rapidly, Selena continued to treat him like a slave, ordering him around in a way which she could see clearly puzzled Bronwen, when she came to the barn with their coffee one morning.

'He's a grown man, dearie,' Bronwen reproached her 'If you're not careful he could turn on you.'

Selena was annoyed that Bronwen had overheard 'Oh, it doesn't bother him, he doesn't usually take any notice.' Keeping her voice down, she smiled appeasingly as she took the flask and biscuits Bronwen had brought

'Having plenty to do can't be worse for him than sitting brooding, which he tends to do if I don't keep reminding him.'

'Reminding him of what?' Bronwen asked.

'Oh, just this and that,' Selena replied evasively.

Bronwen went away again, looking dubious.

'Come and get your coffee, Nero!' Selena called carelessly, when Bronwen had gone, watching as Max climbed down from his ladder. As he silently accepted his drink she noticed his hands. He had good hands, well shaped and always beautifully kept without being effeminate. Now the skin was roughened with cuts and callouses, the nails stained, and torn, no longer immaculate. Weakly Selena wondered why the sight of them should hurt her so.

Ashamed of such weakness, she asked sharply, 'Don't you ever wash?'

He saw her eyes fixed on his hands and was quick enough to understand. 'It's the frost and the kind of work we're doing.' Dryly he added, 'Bronwen suggested I should borrow your barrier cream.'

'Who's going to pay for it?' she snapped.

Again the taut look of frustration. 'I wasn't going to ask for any,' he replied tersely.

'Just as well,' she retorted shrewishly, as he replaced his cup on the overturned box which served as a table, as though the coffee no longer interested him.

'I'll get on,' he said, his sombre eyes, which so often used to remind her of chips of blue steel, gazing at her expressionlessly.

'No!' She spoke on a sudden impulse, feeling she couldn't stand another day of having to endure his almost constant regard. 'I've been thinking,' she went on hurriedly, 'that while the weather holds it might be a good idea to begin mending the fence around the meadow and cleaning up the land. You could finish off in here when it rains. Let's go and take a look.'

Without protest Max followed her.

'When did you say you were going to sell the farm?' he asked anxiously, as they toured the boundaries.

'In the spring,' she said abruptly. 'And it's only a smallholding.'

'In spring,' he muttered, suddenly pausing in his long stride to grasp her arm. 'What will I do then?' he asked, frowning.

The quick triumph Selena felt at the alarm in his voice was quickly dispelled by dismay as sparks from his gripping fingers seemed to leap through her entire body. He didn't feel anything, she could see, and irrationally she was filled with resentment. It just proved, she thought fiercely, how all the real feelings must have been on her side.

'I don't know what you'll do then,' she replied indifferently, pulling her arm away from him. 'You can't expect Bronwen and me to look after you for ever. You could always try remembering you were once a man and make some attempt to pull yourself together.'

'Yes.' The red in his cheeks deepened to humble embarrassment as he turned from her and walked on, 'I'm sorry, Miss North, you're quite right. Perhaps when the doctor comes I might ask his advice.'

'What about?'

'About my future, I suppose,' he said grimly.

The fence and the field were both in fairly good order. The fence needed repairing in a few places and tidying up. Max said he would make a start on it right away, although Selena was sure he wouldn't know the first thing about it. The day was cold, but he seemed to enjoy being out and she realised he probably needed the fresh air after being cooped up in the barn for almost a week.

After telling him where he would find some nails and wire, she went back to the house. She had several things to see to and she had promised Bronwen to do some shopping. It might be good to get away from Moor Edge for an hour, even if it was just as far as the village. Suddenly she felt almost suffocated by it.

What had Max meant when he talked of speaking to Dr Lewis about his future? Selena was still dwelling uneasily on this as she sat in front of the sitting room fire after dinner that evening. The room was cosy and she tried not to think of how lonely she felt sitting by herself. Before Max came she had sat with Bronwen in the kitchen after dark. Bronwen declared she didn't feel in her proper place in the sitting-room and wouldn't be persuaded otherwise. Selena knew that Bronwen wondered why she hadn't asked Max to join her, at least occasionally, in here.

Despondently, Selena sighed. She could hear Bronwen and Max talking in the kitchen now. Their voices were faint, but the house was small and she had left the door slightly open. She didn't feel so isolated this way. Once she fancied she heard Max laugh and was startled. She hadn't even seen him smile since he had come to live with them.

The kitchen was not very comfortable and she had taken to leaving the door open until Max went to bed. He was never very late, and she derived a perverse satisfaction from letting him see the glowing fire and how comfortable she was. Tonight, however, he still hadn't come at ten. Suppressing a desire to go and find out what was keeping him, she went to bed herself.

Ten minutes later, coming out of the bathroom in her dressing gown, she bumped right into him. For the second time that day, his hand went out to grasp her, this time to steady her as she stumbled against him. Her senses leaping dangerously, she jerked back. 'Don't ever touch me!' she cried involuntarily.

'I—I'm sorry,' he stammered, accepting the blame for their encounter humbly.

'Don't you ever look where you're going?' she attacked him with an insolence of which she was secretly ashamed. 'Or have you forgotten where your feet are, as well as everything else?'

His skin, which a few hours in the frosty air had

already toughened, took on an even darker hue, and his eyes, which were usually fixed on hers as though mesmerised, began unaccountably to roam over her, taking in her fresh young beauty. She tied her hair back during the day, but tonight it was hanging loose, in a shining cloud about her shoulders, and her eyes were a vivid, unforgettable blue in the pale oval of her face.

'Haven't you ever seen a woman before?' she jeered, trying to conceal her mounting confusion.

'I suppose I must have done,' Max answered unsteadily.

'You don't know what you've done—do you?' she flung back viciously. 'Always you're supposing!'

His eyes were clearly bewildered. 'It was you who suggested I had ten children, Miss North.'

'I was only trying to help!' she shot back untruthfully.

'I see ...' He sounded so diffident she flinched, but then he startled her by putting out a hand to touch her hair, almost as if he couldn't help himself. 'Do you have a boy-friend, Selena?'

'No!' She was shaken by his new temerity. 'I do not. Nor do I want one!'

'But,' he frowned slowly, as though talking to himself, 'you're young—and so beautiful ...'

Her hands clenched. 'I had a bad experience once.'

Anger swelled in her breast as he didn't so much as blink an eyelid. True, his eyes narrowed, in a way so disconcertingly familiar she felt a twinge of fear, but if he appeared to find her confession distasteful, it was obvious he didn't connect himself with it personally.

'I see,' he said, his frown deepening.

'You don't though, do you?' Mysteriously furious, Selena pulled herself from his tightening hands. 'You might pretend to, but you don't see anything at all. You don't let anything through into that thick head of yours because I believe you're frightened of what you might find! You're just half a man, as I was telling you this afternoon, and a despicable one at that!'

'Half a man?' he murmured hoarsely, staring at where her dressing gown was coming apart at the front, only she was too mad to notice. 'Having written me off mentally, are you challenging me to prove I still function physically?'

His voice was silky, it reminded her so much of the old Max, the breath caught in her throat, the shock of it almost more than she could bear. 'Don't worry,' she gasped, choosing her words with more haste than care, 'I'm not asking you to prove yourself in any way at all.'

He replied in low tones, 'But you've made me curious.'

'Curious?'

Suddenly, as if his confused thoughts angered him beyond his usual restraint, Max reached out, jerking her to him. As his arms closed around her, Selena heard Bronwen's warning about him turning on her, ringing in her frightened ears. 'Let me go!' she cried, trying desperately to insert some kind of authority into her wavering voice.

Ignoring her plea completely, he said huskily, 'I've been so busy concentrating on my mind—my lost memory, I haven't considered anything else. Perhaps I should try and find out what I'm capable of in other directions, if I'm to return to a wife and ten kids, Miss—Selena?'

Before Selena could move his mouth came down fiercely on hers, and whatever he had forgotten it wasn't how to kiss. Savagely he ravaged her full, soft lips, as though the sight of them secretly tormented him, but while he set her immediately on fire, she had no idea as to his reactions. The touch of his mouth brought an immediate response and she was amazed and tormented that he was still capable of such seductive mastery.

She tried to fight him, but a helpless moan escaped her as his lips grew bolder, parting hers. Shock wave after shock wave quivered through her trembling body as with bruising ardour Max bound her to him. His arms tightened, his mouth seemed full of a searing hunger, his appetite ravenous as he took all the sustenance he sought. Under his expertise she was rendered quite helpless, the melting softness of her slender limbs no weapon to fight him with.

When he freed her she was swaying on her feet. Unable to speak, she lifted a shaking hand to her bruised and swollen mouth, tears of anger shimmering in her eyes.

Max appeared comparatively unmoved. Only one muscle twitched in the side of his jaw. He might have been turned to stone. 'I'm sorry,' he said dully, his face as haggard as ever it had been, 'I don't suppose you'll let me stay now?'

Selena might have forgiven him if he had confessed to being overcome with emotion, but she could never pardon such cold impassivity. More and more she was convinced that any affection he had had for her had died, after he had fully possessed her. As was quite usual with a lot of men, after this he had lost interest. He didn't know who she was, of course, because of his accident, but emotions surely weren't governed by the mind. Again she realised that her only possible chance of revenge lay in the humiliation he would one day suffer when he became aware of the kind of work he had been forced to do here.

Without answering his moody plea, she turned and left him, slamming the door of her room. Let him sweat for the rest of the night to start with! It would all add to his punishment.

If Selena didn't exactly sweat during the long, dark hours which followed, she found it difficult to rest. Eventually, contemptuous of the clamour of her own disturbed senses, she began devising more methods of tormenting him, small ways by which she might make his life even more unendurable than it was now.

The next morning Max, as pale as herself, apologised

again. If Selena hadn't slept, he looked as if he hadn't either. All his momentary bravado seemed to have disappeared. He looked racked and scourged with pain.

Tersely Selena told him to forget it and get on with his work. He had better finish the fence around the field, she said, dismissing him.

'You haven't forgotten Dr Lewis is coming today?' Bronwen enquired, some time later.

Unfortunately Selena had, and she didn't particularly want the doctor to find Max working in the open on a day like this. It was cold, but instead of being frosty, as it had been yesterday, a thick mist hung over the moors, so dense as to be capable of soaking a man in a very short time.

'I'll go and fetch him,' she said on impulse, but before she could reach the door, the doctor was there, striding through it.

CHAPTER EIGHT

SLIGHTLY disconcerted, Selena halted. 'Nero,' she explained cautiously, 'is outside. I was just on my way to fetch him.'

'Outside?' Dr Lewis's brows rose. 'He's gone for a walk, I suppose, though it's not a good day for it.'

'No,' Selena edged past him carefully, 'but I know where to find him.'

'I'll come with you,' he smiled.

'Wouldn't you rather stay and have a cup of coffee with Bronwen?' she asked, hoping he would.

Bronwen, frowning darkly, didn't speak, and something about her expression seemed to make the doctor decide to stick to his own decision. 'I think it might be better if we all had our coffee together, when we find him. It will give me a chance to observe how he's getting on.'

Feeling her nerves so taut she wanted to scream at them, Selena gave in reluctantly. Why didn't she tell them? They wouldn't be so concerned if they knew what Max had done, she thought tensely.

They found Max in the field, hammering in posts. He was in his shirt sleeves and wet through. His overalls, which were covered with paint, had been discarded, and Selena was aware that he only had the clothes he stood up in.

Dr Lewis glanced at her sharply. 'I thought you said he was out for a walk?'

'I didn't. You jumped to that conclusion,' she answered defiantly. 'Surely a little work won't do him any harm?'

'It's not the work so much as the weather. Hasn't he a coat?' the doctor frowned.

'No.'

'And nothing to buy one with?' Dr Lewis pursed his lips thoughtfully. 'I think you'd better come back to the village with me, Selena, before we go any farther. Few people have enough money, these days, yet whenever the church holds a jumble sale there's often a lot of perfectly good second-hand clothes which nobody seems to want. I have quite a pile stored in a spare room waiting for the next sale, and I'm sure no one will mind if I borrow a few things for a patient of mine.'

So it was that Selena returned to Moor Edge later with a suitcase full of clothes. The doctor had actually chosen them and they were all in good order, although he feared they might be a little on the small side. His real purpose, he disclosed, in bringing Selena along had been to acquaint her with the layout and workings of the surgery, more than anything else, for when she began her new job with him.

Max was so grateful for the clothes that she suddenly realised how the lack of them must have bothered him. Yet when she thought of all the fine suits he possessed, she found it difficult to believe he could be so pleased with such rough, ill-fitting garments. They couldn't be described in any other way, even if, as the doctor had declared, some of them appeared to have been very little worn.

The next morning, when the doctor arrived to complete the visit which had been cut short the day before, Max thanked him. As they sat around the kitchen table having coffee, Dr Lewis nodded his approval of the warm tweed jacket Max was wearing, then began chatting casually of other things. He touched on several subjects and places, while Selena held her breath, but it soon became clear that nothing of what he said held any meaning for Max. It was quite obvious that he still couldn't remember anything. Yet his fundamental, quick intelligence was still there, along with his old ability to talk well and hold his audience riveted. Listening to him,

Selena stirred uneasily. How was it that he could make even the grass growing in the fields sound interesting? She could see Dr Lewis was puzzled by him, and impressed.

It was arranged that Selena should begin working for the doctor on the following Monday, and after discussing this the doctor left. Because of his morning and evening surgery her working day was to be split into shifts, consisting of roughly three hours each, five days a week. On her first morning, before leaving, she handed Max a list of the things he was to do before she returned, and he promised humbly to do his best.

As the days went by and he was obviously almost killing himself to complete the amount of work she demanded of him, her sense of power grew out of all proportion. So, also, did the length of her lists.

'There's no need for it!' Bronwen protested. 'What are you trying to do to the poor man, dearie? Yesterday he would barely agree to stop for a bite of lunch, and even then he would only take a sandwich.'

'He's lucky to get that!' Selena replied tartly. 'After all, he has no money.'

'And I expect you worry about that, Miss Selena.' Bronwen sighed, clearly of the belief that this was the reason for Selena's hardness with Max. Selena was so tender-hearted over everything else. 'Couldn't he ask the Social Security people for help? At least they might be able to advise him?'

'He doesn't want that kind of help,' Selena assured her coldly, forbearing to mention that she took five pounds each week for his keep from the money Max had given her on that last fateful morning at Lynton. She hadn't wanted to take anything, but Bronwen's savings, when Selena had enquired closer, hadn't amounted to a hundred pounds, which Selena had refused to touch. The five pounds and the work he was doing would undoubtedly salve Max's conscience one day, she thought regretfully, believing that day wouldn't come for a long time yet. So far, Max's memory showed no signs of returning.

While Selena quite enjoyed her new job, she didn't look forward to her long walk home in the dark. It did give her a chance to relax after the bustle of evening surgery, but any benefit she gained was quickly dispelled by the shuttered bleakness of Max's face and the reproach in Bronwen's when she arrived back at Moor Edge. The doctor had offered to run her home, but often he had to go out to an urgent case after surgery, and Selena felt she couldn't ask him to risk the springs of the only car he possessed on the roughness of the road.

Then to her surprise, Max began coming for her. 'We worry about you, Bronwen and I,' he said hesitantly, when she asked why.

'You don't have to,' she retorted crossly, shrugging off the hand he put out to guide her over a particularly rough patch of the track. She didn't have to feel guilty when he winced, she told herself. He was the last person on earth she need feel guilty about!

'Why don't you like me to touch you?' he asked abruptly, one evening, startling her with his unexpected boldness. Not that such a question, couched with such meekness, could be described as bold, exactly, but it was something he had never dared before. Just once had he acted outside his present character. Her pulse throbbing, Selena's thoughts jerked back to the incident outside her bedroom door, when he had kissed her. But he had never attempted to touch her since.

Yet, because even to recall this affected her so alarmingly, she tried to hurt him as much as she could. 'I've told you before, you lack imagination, Nero. Why do you suppose a girl like me despises a tramp like you?'

'Don't call me that!' he said harshly, as if something inside him rebelled at last. 'Oh,' he added bitterly, 'I agree I might only be a tramp, not fit to lick your boots, but I hate that name!' His voice tortured, he confessed, 'Lately I've been hearing another—somewhere in my head, almost on the tip of my tongue. Oh, God!' he groaned, pausing in the darkness to run a weary hand over his head, 'why can't I remember?'

Fear made Selena start like a wild thing in the night. Instinctively she knew she had only to say 'Max.' This brought such a wave of apprehension she reacted vehemently. 'For goodness' sake don't start going all sensitive on me!' she cried. 'What does it matter what a low creature like you is called, but if you don't like Nero, I don't mind calling you something else? I didn't christen you that in the first place. It was your nurses, in hospital.'

Dully he subsided, the angry glitter in his eyes fading. 'I'm sorry. I know it isn't your fault, and as you say, what does it really matter whether I'm Tom, Dick or Harry?'

Where had he got that? A prick of disquiet making her shiver, goaded her to taunt him some more. 'What did your girl-friends call you, I wonder?'

He had control of himself now and merely sighed, well used to her tauntings. 'It must be a long time ago, so I might be excused for not remembering that. And I guess after I'd given my wife ten kids she wouldn't be calling me darling any more.'

'Can't you ever forget I said that!' Angrily Selena stamped her foot on the hard frosty ground. Yet the way he talked worried her. While his jokes might be on the rough side, she recognised a flare of his old caustic wit. His name mightn't be coming back, but she was sure something was.

She was more convinced than ever when he said dryly, 'I don't suppose it would be much use suggesting you called me darling—you said you wouldn't mind.'

'No, I would not!' she retorted furiously. 'I'll never call you that again!'

Silently infuriated, she walked on without pausing to wonder why he suddenly frowned.

This wasn't a row of major proportions, but their next one was. The days went by with Max sinking back into his usual despondency. On the morning after they quarrelled he apologised, as usual, begging her forgiveness with a strained humility she tried hard not to let disturb her. Yet, in spite of his tormented thoughts, physically she knew he looked fitter and harder than ever he had been. When she glanced in the mirror it seemed to Selena that she was the one who grew paler and anxious, as she was continually beset by doubts about the future.

Max had the place in extremely good order, soon there would be little for him to do. At the moment he was busy filling in holes in the road from a heap of gravel which they had discovered almost covered with grass. Selena had thought it was just a natural hillock until Max had investigated. Afterwards Bronwen told them it was a heap of gravel Miss Hartley had ordered and never used. Max had suggested that if the road was repaired, Selena might be able to go to work on the bicycle which he had found and repaired in a shed. It would save her time as well as a long walk several times a day.

She had watched him working on the road with mixed feelings. When she had first taken him in she hadn't thought of anything beyond revenge. Now, after several weeks, she was beginning to have regrets. While she didn't regret making him suffer, she found herself increasingly worried over what was going to happen to them all. Sometimes in the evenings, while sitting in lonely state in front of the sitting-room fire, she found bewildered tears running down her cheeks. Lately she had been forced to recognise that the old saying about revenge being sweet was absolute fallacy. Whatever revenge achieved it certainly did nothing to soothe an aching heart.

Feeling as she did about everything, Selena was in no mood to be tolerant when Max made another sugges-tion. He proposed that it might be a good idea to get some livestock for the fields and some chickens for the barn? He mentioned this when he came to meet her after surgery.

The night was particularly cold and wet, which might have been partially responsible for her turning on him like a virago. 'Do I have to remind you that we have no money?'

'I didn't forget,' Max answered steadily, as if de-termined for once to stand up to her anger. He went on to say he had been talking to one of their neighbours, a farmer who had said he would be willing to rent the field if Max would look after the stock.

'What would you know about looking after sheep or cattle?' she asked sarcastically.

'Not much,' he admitted, 'but I believe all Armstrong wants me to do is count them occasionally.'

'It wouldn't be feasible, anyway,' she replied stub-bornly, 'not when I'm selling as soon as possible.'

'Couldn't you change your mind about selling?' Anxiously pleading, he caught her arm. 'I've finished almost all I can do here, but if I could manage to get work elsewhere, to earn something each week, wouldn't it be possible to keep Moor Edge?'

Selena's heart lurched painfully. Didn't he realise what he was asking? Because she dared not even think of it, she forced herself to point out scornfully, 'What kind of work would you be likely to get, with your memory?'

'I'm not sure, Selena.' It was the first time he had called her that for some time. 'I didn't intend aiming too high. I'm quite aware of my own limitations, but I believe someone would employ me in much the same kind of work as I'm doing now. If you could only learn to like me a little, I'm sure we could all be very happy together.'

'I could never like you,' she cried, alarmed that for one wild moment she had found herself even considering his suggestion. There'd be hell to pay, as it was, without having the additional crime of allowing him to labour for someone else heaped on her head. 'No,' she reiterated hysterically, 'I could never like you. You ought to know that by now.'

'Yes.' There was the dullness of defeat in his voice, but no reproach. 'Don't worry, I could never accuse you of raising false hopes. I've tried hard to please you, but I realise you'll never see me as anything else but a nuisance.'

Something about him caught at Selena's heart and she hated the sensation of remorse. Pain clutched at her along with a terrible awareness of him which seemed to threaten to tear her apart. Why couldn't she get over this hunger to be in his arms, to feel his mouth crushing down on hers? Was there to be no end to her own foolish madness? If she could forget about this and concentrate harder on making Max suffer, would she not be pursuing the wisest possible course, as well as doing her own sex a good turn if he emerged a reformed character?

Yet when she was about to reply sharply, the haggard frustration in his face stopped her. 'Let's get home,' she muttered abruptly instead. 'We're both getting wet.'

At the house he informed her rather belatedly that Bronwen had gone to bed with the cold she had been suffering from all week. He added that he believed he might have caught one, too, as he felt a bit grim.

Glancing at him quickly as they came into the kitchen, Selena saw he was pale. In spite of his increased toughness the bones of his face stood out almost visibly under his tanned skin. His mouth was drawn harshly and his eyes looked sunken. He had aged perceptibly, she realised suddenly, in the weeks he had been here, and while this should have afforded her great satisfaction she felt only recurring twinges of guilt.

Because she hated feeling this way, she snapped impatiently, 'Hadn't you better go and change, then, while I pop up and see if Bronwen wants anything? If you get 'flu I don't know who's going to nurse you.'

Without a word he glanced at her and went off to do as he was told. When she returned from making Bronwen comfortable he was back in the kitchen. The doctor had left him a good supply of clothes, but as the rain had scarcely stopped all day, he had already changed twice. Now, apparently, all he had left was a pair of pants which were much too tight and short. They gave him the appearance of a tall, menacing pirate, the barefoot, dark-visaged kind Selena had seen in pictures. Barely fastening around the waist, the pants clung to his strong, muscular thighs so closely she felt hot colour flooding her cheeks. This embarrassment, if that was what it was, she strove to hide with mocking laughter.

'Have you any idea how very silly you look?' she jeered, making no attempt to stiffle her half hysterical giggles.

The explosion which followed her taunting remark was so unexpected she was struck dumb for several seconds.

'I know damn well how I look!' Max's eyes glittered so brilliantly with fury that she shrank back. Dry-lipped, she tried to apologise, but before she could he ground out. 'You should be grateful, though. It gives you yet another chance to laugh at me, throw more insults in my face.'

'I——' Selena began, her eyes dilating.

His pause was only momentary. Ruthlessly he cut her off, his glance lancing right through her. 'You don't care, do you? I could rot in hell and you wouldn't give me another thought! Don't you know, have you no conception of what it means to lose your memory? It's like being blind mentally, like having to begin from the

cradle again but with no loving parents to help. It's like
fighting with a blank wall every way you turn, but about
worst of all is the worry eating away at your guts over
things you should be aware of. Yes,' he threw at her
savagely, 'your joke about a wife and family might have
worn thin, but I could easily have them. It seems quite
possible that a man of my age might have someone desperately in need of him.'

'People would have made enquiries,' she stammered,
her face white, more shaken than she cared to admit by
his passionate outburst.

'How would you know?' he asked fiercely. 'I could
have walked out on someone, couldn't I? I must have
done something like that to be found wandering without
a penny on me. I could have left my family, threatening
never to come back. They might be needing me—and in
need.'

'There—there are various organisations specially designed to help such people,' she faltered, sweat breaking
out on her brow.

'Are there?' He sounded far from reassured. If anything the suppressed violence in his voice increased as
he glared at her. 'And you think organisations, money,
can make up for the human factor? Would a woman
rather have hard cash, do you think, than a man to
hold her in his arms at night?'

That stung so badly Selena nearly cried out. Didn't
he realise how he had spoiled her for marriage, if this
was what he meant, or any close relationship? It took a
lot of control not to hurl such an accusation bitterly at
him. Anger made her feel sick. 'You can take it from
me that no one's likely to be missing you. You couldn't
be loving or faithful if you tried.'

'You sound very very sure of your facts!' he snapped
back, staring at her curiously.

For a few seconds Selena stood there frozen, aware of
the danger in allowing temper to get the better of discretion but Max's anger frightened her and she wasn't

sure how to cope with it. He looked like a man nearing
the end of his tether. Intuition warned her not to goad
him any further.

It took a lot of effort to put some strength into her
voice. Her lips were suddenly trembling so much she
found it difficult to get anything past them. 'I'll make
you a hot drink,' she said at last, 'then I'd advise you to
go straight to bed. An early night might do you good,
and I'm sure you'll feel less sorry for yourself in the
morning.'

How much more could she stand? Selena wondered,
as she trudged to work next day, after taking Bronwen
breakfast. She had thought she could carry her plans
regarding Max through to the bitter end, now she wasn't
so sure. To start with she hadn't believed it would be
long before his memory returned, but he didn't seem to
be getting any better. When he did have odd flashes of
recollection apparently coming through she was terrified.

This morning he had been quiet again, but for the
first time he hadn't apologised. He hadn't talked at all,
and somehow his silence had frightened her. He had
asked about Bronwen, but nothing else. Bronwen, still
far from well, had stayed in bed. It might be a good
idea, Max had suggested, to ask the doctor to come and
have a look at her. If necessary, Selena resolved, as she
hurried along the road, she would ask to be excused
evening surgery as Bronwen certainly needed proper
attention. Perhaps Dr Lewis's old assistant, who was
anxious to return as her new husband had lost his job,
would be willing to step in.

Dr Lewis did come, and said Bronwen would be
better to remain in bed for a few days. She had a cold
and was a little run down. And yes, he would have a
word with Jenny, who he was sure would help out at
the surgery, thus freeing Selena to stay at home.

Later in the afternoon Max asked if Selena could
spare the time to take a look at the end of the track,

where it joined the main road. He would appreciate her advice, he said.

He was so haggard this afternoon that while she had no inclination to go anywhere with him, she felt a sudden compassion gnawing so fiercely at her heart she was unable to refuse. It was one of those moments when she wanted feverishly to wrap her arms around him and comfort him, something she could never allow herself to do.

Reluctantly, because of the intensity of a longing she must ignore, Selena nodded. 'I'll just tell Bronwen where I'm off to and get my hat,' she said, 'if you'll just wait a moment.'

The end of the track was so bad she stared at it dubiously. 'A load of tarmac would be the perfect answer.'

'Yes,' Max frowned, glancing at her quickly, as though he knew better than to suggest she ordered some. 'I thought if I took some stones from that old wall beside the barn and broke them up, it would be better to fill in the holes with that before putting the gravel down.'

Selena, realising at once that this was the only sensible alternative, sighed. 'You could have done it without my advise, surely?'

'And give you another excuse to vent your temper on me?' he retorted harshly.

Indignant, she stared at his dark face, the glowering eyes which seemed to be eating her up. 'You sound as if you believe I go round looking for an excuse.'

At his ensuing snarl, she backed away as he advanced. 'Who are you trying to fool, Selena? Perhaps I should give you proper justification?' While she gasped out a breathless, apprehensive protest, he grabbed hold of her roughly, dragging her to him.

As he held her tightly against him, she began shaking. Unable to move because of the strength of his arms, she wondered frantically what he meant to do next. She was

so breathless she couldn't speak. Did he intend kissing her?
While she feared his kisses, the remembered pressure of
his hard, sensual mouth was something, she realised she
also longed for. Try as she might to prevent it, she found
her senses responding to the dominant vibrations
coming from Max's aroused body. As his mouth found
hers and his hand slid unexpectedly under her jacket to
find her softly rounded breast, her arms crept tightly
around his neck.

Suddenly she froze. She had been too overwhelmed
by Max's nearness to hear the car approaching. It wasn't
until her ears were assaulted by someone loudly calling
his name that she was jerked to a horrified awareness.

'Max!' the voice went on and on, shrill with surprise,
'Max Heger—Selena!'

It was Pearl, and if Selena was forced unmercifully
back to startled reality, she soon realised Max had been
too. As he released her the harsh rasp of his shocked,
indrawn breath was clearly audible.

'Max?' she heard him murmur, like someone awaken-
ing from a bad dream to the incredulous truth. 'Max
Heger!'

Pearl, having been shouting from the car, now got
out, and the slamming of the car door appeared to bring
Max to his senses. Selena could feel, because he was still
so close, his hard body shaking, but otherwise he showed
remarkable composure. The whiteness of his lips, the
dark brilliance of his eyes was obviously shock. When
he had repeated his name his voice had been full of it,
but his control was impressive. There was no doubt in
Selena's mind that he remembered, that Pearl's voice
had brought everything racing back. There had
undoubtedly been full recall, but what else? Almost
fainting, Selena tried fearfully to envisage his ultimate
reactions when they were alone.

'Max darling!' Pearl's approaching silhouette, though
shrouded in misty twilight, was only too real. Coyly she
surveyed the two of them, and Selena shuddered to think

of the conclusions Pearl must have jumped to on seeing Max and her wrapped in each other's arms.

'Max,' Pearl went on, coming to a smiling halt by their side, 'what a dance you've led us—we've been looking everywhere, although we all guessed what had happened. At least,' she qualified happily, 'I did—and your sister, Max. None of your other friends would believe it.'

'Believe what?' Selena whispered hoarsely, when Max didn't speak.

'That he'd allow any woman to delay his next production.' Still smiling, her glance fluttered back to Max, but now with a hint of apology. 'Actually we haven't been hunting you out. Anyway, I imagined you'd be in a much more glamorous place than this. You did mention this area, though, as the location for the first part of your new film, and a few of us decided to pass a few days looking it up. That's why we were crawling along so slowly. I almost died with shock, I can tell you, when I spotted you standing here.'

'This is the road to the house I inherited,' Selena stammered, praying Max would say something. Anything would be better than such black silence!

'Well, I never!' Pearl laughed. 'Do you know I'd forgotten all about it, but I might have guessed. Right under our very noses! Are you married?'

As Pearl's eyes searched curiously for Selena's left hand, they were joined by her friends from the car. All members of the cast for Max's new film, Selena noted, and all equally curious.

'No, we are not, even if we look it.' Max spoke at last, the derisiveness in his voice giving the impression that he considered the question stupid.

No one replied, or appeared surprised, although Selena, through a haze of embarrassment, noticed one or two cynically raised eyebrows.

Pearl reacted with sophisticated amusement, her glance mockingly spiteful on Selena's red face. 'Sorry I asked,' she murmured sweetly. Then, 'Do you know your father's in London, Selena? He's got a part in the film too.'

'Look,' Max, cold and pale, addressed them curtly, 'why don't you all go on to your hotel and I'll see you there later? I've a cold coming on and I don't feel particular sociable, but I promise I'll try to make it.'

Pearl seemed about to protest, then she agreed reluctantly. After naming a hotel, she pouted at Max prettily. 'You won't disappear again, will you? I can still have my part?'

'Yes,' Max nodded, 'most definitely. And I certainly don't intend disappearing again. I hope to start work immediately.'

Watching expressionlessly, as their unexpected visitors piled in their car and departed, Max said, his voice icy with anger. 'I'm relieved they decided to go at once. Otherwise they might have seen me strangle you.'

His quietness was somehow more frightening than if he had shouted. Hate leapt out of his eyes and he looked as if he could have slain her on the spot. The force of his contempt hit her so harshly she was unable to say a word. Nor could she seem to manage even the slightest gesture in her own defence as he grasped her arm and began dragging her along the track.

'Don't!' she cried, feeling her arm might well be drawn out of its socket. Wholly agonised, she was so full of terrified despair she couldn't think straight. She knew some desperate kind of release that the need to pretend she didn't know who Max was no longer existed, that it was over before the strain had become past bearing. But any such relief was quickly dispelled by his fury. This, combined with her fears that the temporary shock of discovery might have driven him half out of his mind, made her stumble and fall weakly to her knees.

'Please, Max!' she gasped, as he continued to drag her mercilessly through the gravel and mud.

It could have been the utterance of his name, falling so easily from her trembling lips, which broke the final thread of his self-control. He stopped, but only to haul her roughly to her feet. As she swayed before him he lifted his hand and slapped her cruelly, twice across the face. When, with a cry of pain, she shrank back from him, his hard mouth curved in a mirthless, tigerish grin, while his eyes glittered darkly as they bored into hers.

'If I didn't hit you I'd kill you, which is what you really deserve. Think of it that way, then you might not hurt so much.'

'Max . . .'

'Yes, Max!' he snarled, holding her shocked gaze contemptuously. 'How easily you manage to say it now! Yet you chose to call me by a name I detested. Unfortunately I can't kill you, but I'm going to teach you a lesson you won't ever forget.'

'If you'd only listen, Max!' she could hear her own voice shaking as she tried to get through to him. He couldn't realise what he was saying!

At once she was made to understand that he wasn't prepared to listen. 'To think I was once attracted to a girl with a mind as twisted as yours!' he raged savagely, as he began shaking her, all the time snapping out insults until her ears rang and she felt so sore and distracted she scarcely knew what she was trying to say any more. It was almost dark, but the darkness wasn't nearly so frightening as the bitter hatred in Max's face.

'Why did you do it?' he thundered, pausing at last.

'I could ask you the same thing,' she countered desperately, between sobs.

'What the hell are you talking about?' he shot back.

'That—that you should ask that!'

'I am asking it!' he exploded. 'Let's get my supposed sins out of the way, by all means, before I start on yours. Just what are you accusing me of?'

Blindly she stared at his smouldering face. How dared he persist so? Even now she went hot to remember. Her voice rising on a note of tortured hysteria, she cried, 'I was unconscious. How would I know what happened, exactly? But I was able to read your despicable note next morning, which left me in little doubt . . .'

'You little fool!' Momentarily he was obviously stunned, but not enough to subdue his scornful rage.

'Oh, I realised I'd been all kinds of a fool,' she choked, 'but not until it was too late. By then you'd conveniently disappeared. But don't worry, I kept the money you left to salve your conscience. I had no option when I couldn't find you to return it, but it's all there—that is, apart from a few pounds I've spent on your keep. Did you think I would touch it?'

'I didn't touch you!' he ground out.

Her eyes stretching with shock in the whiteness of her face, Selena suddenly drew a hoarse breath. 'You mean . . .?'

'Oh, come off it!' His mouth tightened with derision. 'You've never slept with a man before, that I did discover. If I'd made love to you that night, you'd certainly have known next morning.'

'Oh . . .' As, instinctively, she knew he spoke the truth, her face flooded wildly with colour. All this time he had allowed her to believe, let her suffer! 'Why, you're diabolical!' she cried, her hand flying out furiously, driven by anger. It was caught and held before it had time to contact the hard cheek it aimed at, but she was too distraught to notice. 'The money,' she breathed raggedly. 'Why did you leave that if you didn't do anything?'

'Simply to punish you a little, until you had time to think it out,' Max jibed. 'Don't you think you deserved something after the dance you'd led me? I meant you to have a few anxious moments. How was I to know you'd be such a gullible little fool?'

'You might keep calling me that, but you're a monster!' she moaned, forgetting her own part in the matter, as well as the subsequent lengths she had allowed her thirst for revenge to drive her to.

Max hadn't, though. 'That's nothing to the way I'd describe you! All these weeks pretending not to know who I was, treating me like dirt, making me do the roughest work you could find. To say nothing of wasting my time.' His voice lowered to a menacing snarl as she shivered convulsively. 'They say, my dear, that hell hath no fury like a woman scorned, but you'll find a man's retaliation can be just as painful. Before I'm through with you, I'll see you crawl!'

White to the lips, she stared at him. 'Max, I'm—I'm sorry. I realise I should have told you, but it was solely because of what I believed you'd done to me. I never thought . . .'

'And now it's a bit too late,' he cut in harshly. 'God, I could . . .' Swiftly he let go of her and she realised at once that she feared he was going to be ill.

'Max!' she whispered, as he turned to lean over a nearby fence, her own stomach churning with a strange mixture of pity, fear and remorse. He was bound to suffer some physical reaction. Again she regretted the part she had played, but she had never dreamt his memory would return so abruptly. A deep anxiety for him struck her, along with the knowledge that she had acted despicably, and all for no purpose. Yet how could she have known? As she hurried anxiously to his side, she tried to take no notice of a small voice that whispered that if she hadn't been so much in love with him, she might have been able to assess certain things more rationally. Yes, she thought hollowly, she loved him, but it was the one thing he must never find out. Not now.

CHAPTER NINE

As Selena approached she saw Max was leaning against a tree, his head in his hands. Savagely, as she paused beside him, he thrust her away, his face ravaged with shock. Obviously reaction was hitting him harder than he had expected; he looked terrible.

Resolutely she tried not to feel more frightened than she already was. 'How do you feel, Max? What do you remember?' she asked tremulously, forgetting her own anguish immediately to dwell on his.

'I remember everything.' He ignored her tearful sympathy and there was menace in his voice as he reached out to jerk her swiftly to him again. 'Almost everything came back soon after Pearl arrived. Almost the instant she called my name.'

'I'm sorry——' Selena began helplessly.

'Not half as sorry as you're going to be!' Anger almost visibly leaping from him, he grasped a handful of her long, windblown hair to pull her head quickly against his broad shoulder. Then his mouth was assaulting hers ruthlessly, brutally grinding into the trembling softness of her lips until she moaned in agony. Still holding her tightly, he thrust her sweater aside, so that his hands could roughly caress her throbbing breasts, while his mouth continued to plunder her face and throat.

'Don't tell me you don't like me doing this to you,' he muttered harshly.

Frantically she tried to deny it, but pain and ecstasy intermingled so indiscernibly it proved her undoing. Resistance was impossible as, her denial infuriating him, Max moulded her in his hands until she became totally submissive to his every movement. While the demands of his hard searching mouth might be threatening to stop her breathing, his deep, passionate kisses seemed to be taking her to unbelievable heights. Suddenly, blindly, with a choked little cry, Selena found herself clinging to him.

Yet, despite the excitement he was cruelly arousing, she was swaying under a darkness which threatened to engulf her when at last Max lifted his head.

'Your level of endurance will have to rise,' he mocked acridly, as he released her, 'if you're to survive until my desire for revenge is sated.'

Pressing a hand to her bruised mouth, in an effort to restrain a feverish sob, she retreated a step, trying to get out of the range of his hard, virile body.

'Max,' she begged, finding herself concentrating on his problems again, rather than her own, 'I think you should come back to the house and let me call Dr Lewis. You must need some attention—you've had a dreadful shock.'

'Have I?' he sneered, but he did turn and begin striding up the road. When Selena paused, with the obvious intention of running to the village, his hand grasped her arm with its former vicious grip. 'You're coming with me! I don't want you fetching Lewis here. Naturally I'll tell him I've recovered, when I see him, but physically, after the initial surprise, I don't feel any different. He knows my memory has been returning, anyway.'

'You never told me.' She was having to run to keep up with him and she thought bitterly that it might be true what he said about his physical condition.

'It was only odd things,' he snapped. 'Nothing to really go on.'

'Such as?'

'God, do you never give up! Such as when you said you'd never call me darling again. I wondered about that until something almost came through. Even without Pearl's timely arrival, I believe I would soon have had complete recall.'

'You gave Pearl the part she wanted after all?' she

panted, her mind veering irrationally.

'Yes,' he replied curtly, 'and your father, after Pearl contacted him about something and advised him to get in touch with me.'

'I had no idea,' Selena returned bleakly.

'You weren't there to tell.'

Suddenly she felt uneasy about this. There was something she didn't understand. Remembering her first reaction when she had found Max on her doorstep all those weeks ago, she asked the question which had bothered her then.

'Why did you leave the States so soon?'

He answered immediately, but his voice was guarded. 'I simply decided to swap my itinerary around. I had various important things to see to here.'

'Deciding the exact location for your film must have been one of them?'

'Yes, that.' He kicked open the house door and dragged her into the kitchen. Once inside, he pulled out a chair and with a smothered groan slumped with his head in his arms across the table. His shoulders were bent and she saw the sinews on the back of his hands were tense.

'Max?' she whispered, concerned for him despite his fury, and the amount she suspected still waiting to be poured on her defenceless head. 'Max,' she repeated, when he took no notice of her urgent plea, 'are you feeling worse again?'

'Not really.' He sat up at last, staring at her. 'I just need a little time to pull myself together, then I'll be ready to deal with everything.'

This, sounding more like a threat than anything else, caused her to shiver.

'I could certainly do with a drink,' he said grimly, as she stood regarding him warily.

This made Selena realise she must be suffering from some degree of shock herself, otherwise she would already have been making him some hot, sweet tea. 'I'll put the kettle on,' she said quickly.

'Not that kind of drink!' he grated.

'There's nothing else here, as you know.'

'We'll soon alter that,' he promised grimly.

About to grab the kettle, Selena halted abruptly, as what he said seemed to thrust her into a future strewn with pitfalls. 'I suppose you'll be leaving right away?' she asked, wondering how she could feel both hopeful and despairing at the same time.

'I'll leave when it suits me.' His eyes ran over her with cold deliberation.

Completely dismayed, Selena met his sneering glance with more than a hint of desperation. 'It would be much easier if you went at once, otherwise what will we tell Bronwen? How much do you intend telling her?' Beseechingly she searched his impassive face. 'You let Pearl believe,' she accused him wildly. 'At least, I believe Pearl believes . . .'

'Shut up!' he sliced through her stammering words, curtly cutting off her incoherent pleas. 'I can see quite clearly where your bloody insanity has led to, without your trying to explain it. I know damn well what Pearl thinks, and the rest of the crew by now, I imagine, and I couldn't care less!'

'But your film?' she whispered, aghast at his attitude, even if he had some justification.

'What about my film?' he rasped, getting to his feet, to tower over her as she shrank against the stove.

'You can't make it here.'

'Why can't I?' His face was so harsh with fury she could almost feel it. 'I have to sleep somewhere.'

'Your bed . . .' She was about to point out its obvious discomfort, but somehow couldn't find the courage to remind him of that.

His eyes glinting, Max took up where she left off. 'I agree, it's not the best, but I can always use yours, from now on.'

'Mine?' Heat flooded her cheeks painfully as she trembled.

'Don't worry,' he drawled savagely, 'I don't intend joining you in it. A straight swap will suit me fine.' While she stared at him speechlessly, he enlightened her further. 'The same goes for your parlour. I'll take that over as well, while you employ yourself here, as I've had to do in the past, in the kitchen. Bronwen is certainly going to need all the help she can get during the next few weeks. When I come home each evening I shall require a good meal, a good fire and privacy.'

'You can't make me do it,' she cried in panic. 'I'll tell my father!'

'Go ahead,' he jeered contemptuously. 'Feel free to discover how much help you can expect from him. One word of warning, though, before you start. If he should be rash enough to take any notice of your whining complaints, both he and Pearl are out! Call it blackmail or whatever you like, but it's a fact.'

'My father mightn't mind,' she gasped, stunned by the lengths Max seemed determined to go to.

'I think you'll find he will, especially since his wife is pregnant.'

'Babs?' Shocked, Selena stared at him, her eyes stretched wide, 'You can't be serious! She—she's only thirty—but . . .'

As her voice trailed off in shock, Max's mouth curled. 'Don't you think it's natural for married people to want babies? They seem happy enough about it, but they're obviously going to need all the financial help they can get.'

'You fiend!' she cried, feeling sick.

'Fiend?' His black brows rose cynically above coldly furious eyes. 'Don't you think you should be calling yourself that? Look at my hands, for instance—feel them,' he rubbed them roughly down the sides of her face. 'I wouldn't have a workman on a set with hands like these.'

Selena looked at his hands with undisguised shame. It

seemed pointless to say she was sorry when she had known all along what was happening.

'I'm not ashamed of them,' he snapped impatiently, 'nor so effeminate I can't bear the sight of them, I'm merely using them to demonstrate the lengths you were prepared to go to, in case you'd forgotten. In your thirst for revenge you couldn't make the work rough enough. You couldn't contain your amusement, either, at the sight of my ill-fitting clothes.'

'Well, you were partly to blame,' she retorted unwisely, knowing it was either temper or tears.

Max stared back at her, his mouth grim. 'Right, I'll grant you that, even if you drove me to act as I did. And if you'd allowed yourself a week, say, to pretend you didn't know me, I might have called quits. But two months—God, how bigoted can you get! When I think of how hard I tried to please you—I must have been mad!'

Selena turned her head with a suppressed sob, unable to produce another word in her own defence. She felt so miserable and unhappy she was sure she was in danger of breaking down completely, and whatever else she did she mustn't do that. She could have wept with relief when, with a look of total disgust, Max said he was going upstairs. Perhaps he, too, saw no sense in continuing such a painful interview indefinitely.

When he was gone she went as he had done and slumped across the kitchen table. Whichever way she looked she could only see chaos. In spite of being glad of a brief respite, she still had so much to sort out, her head reeled. Max had promised he would make her crawl and she didn't doubt it. She had seen him in action before, in London, and he was quite impressive, but she failed to see any sense in prolonging the situation between them. Max had his faults, but she could have sworn he wasn't a vindictive man, yet all he seemed able to think of was revenge. She could only hope bleakly that by the morning he might have seen sense.

He wasn't gone long. When he came down again he told her curtly, 'I'll send a taxi for you. It should be here in half an hour.'

Blankly she lifted her head. 'You—you can't be thinking of walking to the village, after what you've just been through. You can't be well enough!'

'I assure you I am and I can,' he snapped. 'There's nothing wrong with me now, thank goodness, and I've weathered many a worse crisis than this. I doubt if you will, but that's another matter.'

With a painful flicker of fear in her breast, she met his smouldering grey eyes. Swallowing it down, she licked her dry lips. 'If you must go out tonight, Max, let me run down to the village and send a taxi back for you. I'm not going anywhere.'

'No, thanks,' he was adamant, 'and you are going somewhere. Just be ready when your transport arrives.'

'You don't need me,' she protested.

'I don't,' he agreed shortly, 'but I want you with me.'

'Why?' She glanced at him with sudden anger. 'Just so everyone can stare and speculate as to what's been going on? Don't you think things are bad enough as it is? If I did come I'd refuse to talk to anyone,' she threatened shakily.

'It won't be necessary for you to say anything,' Max assured her coldly.

Her heart full of trepidation, she gave up, the aftermath of such a devastating afternoon fast overtaking her. Unevenly she said, 'There's one thing you haven't thought of—Bronwen. How can we leave her?'

'She'll take no harm for an hour. Take her a light supper and tell her I've recovered my memory. She'll be quite satisfied with that, you'll find.'

'How about your clothes?' Selena, refusing to be so easily beaten, searched desperately for anything that might keep him at home. Hopefully she glanced at the borrowed sweater and trousers he wore. They, unfortunately, didn't look too bad, not with his renewed

air of arrogance. In fact some might consider his slightly
more rugged appearance merely added to his attraction.

'What about my clothes?' he rapped indifferently.
'I'll have my own brought from London tomorrow, but
these are quite comfortable, even if they no longer
appear to arouse your amusement.'

Flinching from his hard sarcasm, Selena heard herself
asking, 'The night you came here, you didn't have a
jacket and the police never found one. They couldn't
find your car, either. Can you remember what happened
to it!'

Max's voice was clipped and cool. 'When I left
London I had a jacket, but I didn't bring a car. I had,'
he paused tautly, 'a very important document on me
which I presume my assailants must have taken when
they helped themselves to my coat.'

As Selena nodded and looked at him enquiringly, he
shrugged, not apparently willing to satisfy her curiosity.
Again he hesitated warily. 'I'd found the old house we
intend using in the first part of the film, but I believe I'd
left it rather late. I remember the lights of a car coming
up behind me, but nothing more.'

'That must have been when you were knocked unconscious. Then I suppose you came to and walked
here?' Selena flushed. 'You know the rest.'

'Yes,' he agreed darkly, 'I know the rest.' His eyes
glinting with anger, he seemed tempted to shake her
again, but instead he stepped back. Tightly he said,
'You'd better let me have what you have left of the
money I gave you. It would perhaps make people
speculate a little too much if I turn up tonight without
a penny to my name.'

When she fetched it from the locked bureau in the
sitting-room, he stuffed the whole of it in his pocket
without looking at it. 'You'd better get yourself ready,'
he said flatly. 'We can talk later.'

When the door snapped shut behind him, Selena
began wearily to do as she was told. She prepared

Bronwen a tray and took it up to her and tidied her bed while she ate her supper. As she worked, she mentioned casually that Max's memory had returned. Without elaborating she explained how Pearl had seen him at the end of the road.

Surprisingly, as Max had suggested she might, Bronwen accepted this explanation without suspicion. 'Oh, I am glad!' she exclaimed. 'And to think he's a famous film star!'

'Director,' Selena corrected automatically.

'Well, it's all the same thing, isn't it?' Bronwen smiled happily. 'I always told you, didn't I, that he'd turn out to be somebody?'

'He would like me to go out with him for an hour to meet some of his friends.'

'At this time of night?' Bronwen asked doubtfully.

'Perhaps I should go to make sure he's all right,' Selena replied evasively. 'He says he is, but you can never tell. Once he gets on talking he might forget to come home, if there's no one there to remind him. I don't like leaving you, though.'

Bronwen handed Selena her empty tray. 'You go, dearie, don't worry about me. I've taken one of those tablets the doctor left and I'll probably sleep until morning. I'm only too pleased at the way things have turned out.'

In the kitchen Selena dumped the dishes quickly in the sink and darted up the other staircase to get ready. She only had five minutes left of the half hour Max had allowed, but she might make it if she hurried.

In her room she halted abruptly. Where had all her clothes gone? In the wardrobe, when she wrenched the door open to see if the clean jeans and shirt which she had thought she had left on the chair were there, she found only Max's odd assortment of clothes, hanging in lonely state. It was the same with the chest of drawers. They were empty; all her belongings had disappeared. Her blue eyes darkening with anger, she looked at the

bed. It had been turned down and Max's borrowed
dressing gown was draped over the end of it.

Breathing fire, she rushed to the room next door. Sure
enough, there were her things in a heap on the floor. He
hadn't even bothered to put them neatly away, as he
had done for himself! With a sob she began picking
them up.

So he was already carrying out his threats! Selena's
heart pounded with tearful fury. Recalling the way he
had slapped and kissed her, his rough words and even
rougher handling, she told herself wildly that there was
no need to put up with more.

Then suddenly she recalled her father and Pearl and
remembered what Max had threatened. It must be one
of the oldest forms of blackmail in the world but unfortunately, in this case, there was no escaping it. Selena
wasn't sure if she would have done much for her father
and Pearl, but there was Babs and the baby.

'Oh, God!' she gasped, thinking of having a baby
brother or sister twenty years younger than herself. It
would be a half-brother or sister, but it would still be
family! Why, when it was older, she would be more like
its aunt. And what would Mummy say when she heard?
She must be past the age for having babies, but Selena
doubted if she'd be pleased to hear of her divorced husband's wife having one.

Max had a nerve, though, if he intended her to suffer
more than she had done already. Any relief she felt at
knowing he hadn't possessed her was quickly dispelled
by this new turn of events. At the moment it seemed she
couldn't fight him without hurting her family, such as it
was, but at the first chance she would be gone.

What a dreadful muddle! Selena thought, sluicing the
tears from her face and dressing hurriedly. She could
hear the taxi growling in the yard below, but it would
have to wait. Guessing that most of those there tonight
would be dressed casually, she extracted a pair of jeans
and a shirt from the rest and pulled them on. Over her

slender shoulders she threw a blue sleeveless jacket which toned with the checks in her shirt and the warm scarf around her neck. Her hair, because she hadn't time to do anything with it, she brushed and tied back, and though her mouth was swollen she concealed the bruises with lipstick. Hoping to draw attention from the state of her lips, she tipped the end of her long lashes with a touch of mascara.

The taxi deposited her outside a comfortable country hotel several miles away, without mishap. Thanks to the hard work Max had put in, most of the track to the house was now quite decent. In the hotel, as she was being directed to the lounge, Max came to meet her, holding out a hand. When she put her own behind her back, he snapped between his teeth, 'Play up or you'll be sorry—very sorry, I can tell you!' He bent lovingly to kiss her mouth, slipping off her scarf in a proprietorial manner as he did so.

Above the quickening beat of her heart Selena was aware of the curious glances, the amused quirking of mouths as Max drew her down to sit beside him. After brief introductions, he ordered another round of drinks, then leant closer. His lips dangerously near her ear, he muttered, 'You look about sixteen in that outfit. Couldn't you find something to make you look a bit older?'

'Sorry.' Easing away from him, she smiled maliciously. 'I did search for a few extra years, but you must have thrown them out with the rest of my things.'

'Don't you care for your new quarters?' he asked smoothly, his arm going firmly around her waist, deliberately foiling her efforts to escape him.

'No!' she whispered furiously, wanting to hit him. 'For one thing, the bed . . .'

'Your bed's still big enough for two,' he taunted, to her horror raising his voice slightly, which sent cynical eyebrows soaring even higher.

'You're . . .' The glass of champagne Max placed, with

a glinting smile, against her indignant lips, successfully prevented any further eruptions. Rather than choke, Selena was forced to take a quick gulp of the sparkling wine. Pearl, she noticed, as their glances collided, was as interested as the others, if not so surprised. Vaguely, Selena remembered Pearl declaring Max fancied her a lot. How wrong could one get? she wondered bitterly, morosely considering his hatred. Any impression he meant to give that he and Selena were lovers must just be to cover up his devious activities at Moor Edge.

Wriggling unobtrusively as she might, she couldn't escape his confining arm and was forced to sit by him while he put the finishing touches to a programme of work already drawn up. The producer and designer both appeared to have everything in hand, having apparently faithfully adhered to Max's former instructions. Selena was amazed by his astuteness. He had every small detail at his fingertips. This, after he had been ill so long, she found remarkable. Obviously he hadn't changed his mind about not mentioning his loss of memory, as no one remarked on it. They all appeared to accept that Selena was the reason he had stayed at Moor Edge for so long, and she went hot even to think of it.

'Let me go!' she whispered angrily, when she felt she could stand his close proximity no longer.

'You can go to—you know where,' Max hissed back, 'but not until after I've finished with you.'

Her ear burned. She had never heard him curse as he had done that afternoon and she wished he would stop. It wasn't until he was called unexpectedly to the telephone that she felt free to breathe. This reprieve was shortlived, however, as she was suddenly pounced on by none other than Primo Pleasure.

'What are you doing here?' she gasped, as Primo, as opportunist as ever, dragged her over to a dark corner.

'Aha!' he wagged a playful finger at her. 'I've just arrived this very minute from London. I've got a part in the new Heger film, a knight in shining armour. I'm to have a white charger, too, well equipped to carry you off.'

'I didn't even know you could ride', she exclaimed, for want of something better to say. She wasn't sure she should be standing here with Primo or any other man, seeing Max was in such a nasty temper, but she had to speak to somebody and she'd known Primo a long time.

'There's nothing much I can't do. Just try me, sweetheart.'

Trying to look prim, she tilted her chin. 'I think I'll take your prowess for granted, thank you.'

He gave her a hurt glance. 'You're playing Pearl's maid, aren't you? She told me about it.'

Startled, Selena lowered her eyes quickly. He mustn't have seen Pearl for a while. 'You're not up with the latest news,' she faltered, her lighter mood deserting her again. 'I'm not in the production at all.'

'Oh, no!' he groaned aloud. 'I was banking on it! But,' he asked suspiciously, 'if you aren't in the cast what are you doing here?'

Selena's cheeks went pink and she hoped he wouldn't notice. 'I was left a house not far away which I've been repairing, prior to selling,' she told him.

'Well, isn't that super!' he grinned, not allowing surprise to deter him for a moment as he wrapped an arm around her. 'Now,' he cried dramatically, 'I can get away from it all. When all this becomes too much for me I'll come and see you! We can make love in rustic seclusion, sweetheart.'

Suddenly, as Primo laughed with glee, Selena's shoulder was grasped and she was almost torn from his arms.

Max stood there, his face livid. 'If I ever catch you within miles of Selena or Moor Edge, Pleasure, you'll never know what hit you!'

Primo gulped visibly, his face going all colours. 'I didn't know I was trespassing,' he stammered.

'Never say I didn't warn you.' Max's expression was glacial as he dragged Selena away.

'Where are we going?' she choked, as he swept her from the building.

'Home,' he snapped.

'Home?' her voice rose. 'But I've scarcely had a word with Pearl yet!'

'We have Bronwen to think of,' he reminded her.

'Yes, of course.' She subsided anxiously, but her heart was still beating too rapidly. 'Did you have to give everyone the impression that we're having an affair?' she whispered hoarsely, as they got in the waiting taxi.

'I've always found it pays to be frank with people, rather than keep them guessing,' he replied blandly.

'But I'm not having an affair with you!' she insisted, pain rushing through her that he could be so cruelly blatant. 'Nor do I intend having one,' she added desperately.

'Methinks the lady doth protest too much,' he mocked.

'You're totally unscrupulous!' she hissed.

Max glanced at her sideways, his mouth harshly set. 'I meant what I said to young Pleasure back there, as well.'

Selena shivered afresh with indignation. 'So he's another whose job is to rely on my discretion?'

'It's about time you learnt to be more responsible,' he snarled, as if even to think of Primo Pleasure infuriated him.

She didn't reply. She just sat beside him sullenly until they reached Moor Edge, too aware of both his decisive mind and body. What was the use of feeling so miserable? she chided herself. Why fight him? Wouldn't it be easier to give in, to meekly obey his curt commands? He was too much for her, she could never come to terms with his iron will. Yet that didn't explain the bond which drew them together. It was there all the time, impossible to ignore or deny. It blinded the senses, raced heartbeats, arousing them both to a pitch of unbearable excitement where mere kisses were far from enough.

She must, Selena thought distractedly, learn to control her own too passionate response. Max only wanted to punish her for what she had done, and she shrank from any further involvement with him which might inadvertently betray her completely.

At Moor Edge Max paid off the taxi and told him to return at eight the next morning.

'Where do you think you're going?' Selena demanded sharply, when the man had gone. 'You'll make yourself ill again!'

'It wasn't exactly an illness I was suffering from,' he retorted, steering her into the house. 'But if I do I should be quite comfortable in my new bed, with you at my beck and call.'

Bitterly she looked at him. 'It's no comfort to know I have only myself to blame,' she burst out. 'What a fool I was not to tell Dr Lewis who you were! Then the hospital could have contacted London or Lynton and I need never have seen you again!'

'You're a girl who will always have second thoughts,' he sneered. 'You're far too impulsive.' His face darkened coldly. 'I don't mind impulsiveness so much as lies. You aren't about to tell me you didn't want to see me again?'

Quickly Selena lowered her eyes, reluctant that he should see what she feared might lie in them. 'It seems you wouldn't believe me if I did?' she countered.

'No way!' he grated.

'When I make Bronwen her cocoa, would you like some too?' she asked, unable to bear his cold-blooded baiting.

'No!' he said arrogantly. 'And don't think you can bribe me into a better mood with cocoa, or by ignoring what I say.'

His voice was so caustic she felt like hitting him, but he looked so haggard and pale, in spite of his obvious anger, that she felt concern swamp the hostile retort which rose to her lips. 'Do you really have to go out so early tomorrow, Max?'

'I'm going to London,' he said abruptly, watching as she reached for the milk to heat for Bronwen's cocoa.

Alarmed, Selena's glance flew back to him. 'London?'

'I'm coming back the next day,' he assured her maliciously. 'I have things to see to.'

Well, he would have, wouldn't he, after all this time. Helplessly she bit her lip, which was still so sore she winced. 'I suppose you'll be bringing your manservant back with you?'

'Why should I?' his voice was cool. 'I have you and Bronwen.'

'And my bed!' she couldn't prevent herself from exclaiming angrily. 'I hope you enjoyed yourself throwing all my things out!'

'I was in a hurry,' he excused himself indifferently. 'Would it have made any difference if I'd carried your things out, piece by piece?'

'You're a fiend!' she choked, flushing hotly.

Blandly Max shrugged. 'I've told you I'm quite willing to share the larger room.'

As the heat in her cheeks increased, she realised the futility of arguing with him in the mood he was in. Anger, she sensed, still consumed him to a dangerous degree, and if his taut control went she would be the one to suffer. Cautiously she tried to ignore his last remark, which was clearly meant to incite. 'You weren't even willing to let me speak to Pearl tonight!'

'She threw you out, didn't she?' he snapped, as though this explained it.

Selena was stunned. 'Who told you?'

'So I was right.' His mouth curled in jeering satisfaction.

'How did you find out?'

'A neighbour, when I was enquiring where you—where everyone was. She said—reluctantly, mind you—she was passing the door when she heard Pearl shouting at the top of her voice and a few minutes later saw you stumbling out with a suitcase.'

'It—it didn't happen quite like that,' Selena muttered.

'Near enough. She's a bitch.'

Selena was puzzled. 'If that's your opinion of her why did you change your mind about giving her a part?'

'That has nothing to do with it,' his eyes were suddenly veiled, 'I'd already been in touch with her agent.'

Uncertainly, Selena stared at him, but had nothing sorted out as he added, 'As a matter of fact Pearl is returning to London with me in the morning as she won't be required on the set for another week or two.'

'And my father?'

Max surveyed her anxious face disparagingly. 'He's not in the part of the film which will be shot down here. At the moment he's doing something in the West End, in a night club, I believe, but not for me.'

'I see,' Selena replied dully.

Narrowly, Max went on staring at her. She saw his fingers stretch, then curve into his palms, as if it took a lot of resolution not to take hold of her again and shake her. She heard his breath rasp and there was a hard flush over his cheekbones, but his voice was curt when he spoke. 'I'm off to bed. I'll see you in the morning.'

Which seemed a clear indication that he expected her to be up and have his breakfast ready. Her teeth clenched against an angry rejoinder, she nodded.

'Goodnight, then,' he said coldly.

Before he left next morning, Max gave her explicit instructions that she wasn't to leave Moor Edge until he returned. He was ordering some supplies, he said, and she must be there to receive them or Bronwen might be worried.

He was very concerned over Bronwen of a sudden. Selena watched suspiciously as the taxi which would take him to the station drove away. Of course, she admitted, he had always shown Bronwen great courtesy and helped her all he could. While he might be using her to ensure that Selena didn't stray, Bronwen would be quite safe from his animosity. It was against a much younger woman that he intended venting his spite.

Then, as her conscience pricked her, Selena hung her head in sudden shame. Max was right, she deserved to suffer. If, after a few days, she had confessed to knowing him, or even contrived to let the hospital know anonymously who he was, no one could have actually rebuked her. It must seem she had carried her thirst for revenge to ridiculous lengths. Only now did she suspect she had found it impossible to let him go. Successfully she had managed to disguise love with hatred, the contempt she had managed to display having merely been a cloak to hide her true feelings. Now she was having to struggle against the strength of her own desire, the force of love moving within her like a live thing, which threatened to overcome everything else.

Burying her hot face in her hands, she gave a little moan of despair. How was she to hide how she felt from Max, if he continued to insist that she stayed here with him? She could only hope feverishly that something would delay him in London, even to the extent of ensuring that he never came back.

CHAPTER TEN

THROUGHOUT the day, to Selena's surprise and dismay, supplies actually did begin to arrive. This killed all the hopes she had been nursing that Max might change his mind about living here instead of at the hotel.

First came a deep freeze stocked with meat and vegetables. The man with the van even knew where it was to go. He asked the way to the utility room which adjoined the kitchen, which Bronwen referred to as the washhouse. Next came cartons of food to fill the kitchen cupboards and fridge. A supply of drinks followed these, not an abnormal amount but enough to keep a man happy for several weeks. Selena couldn't think how Max had managed it all in so short a time. It made her shudder to realise that none of his usual ability to get things done must have been in any way impaired by his accident.

Bronwen didn't appear put out when Selena tried to explain that the noise was about. 'I ought to be up soon,' she declared. 'I'll enjoy looking after Mr Heger.'

'He should be comfortable with two of us running after him!' Selena mumbled sullenly, but when Bronwen glanced at her sharply and asked, 'What was that?' she pretended not to have heard her.

Before tea on the following day, Selena went for a long walk over the moors while Bronwen rested. Usually she enjoyed being out of doors and the wildness of the countryside appealed to her. This afternoon, however, the autumn mist and early darkness only added to her depression instead of alleviating it. It didn't help either, when she returned to the house, to find Max was back. He was talking to Doctor Lewis. For one frightening moment she thought something must have happened to

Bronwen while she had been out.

'No,' the doctor smiled as he reassured her, 'I'm just paying both my patients a routine visit, but I don't think you need worry over-much about either of them, especially now that Mr Heger has recovered completely.'

Selena felt her heart beat faster as her glance slid to Max. Dressed in his own well-fitting clothes again, he did indeed look fit and well. His old assurance was back, too. She could see Dr Lewis was impressed.

'I'm going to arrange for Bronwen to have a month in a convalescent home,' the doctor said.

'Oh?' Selena stammered, startled and apprehensive as she suddenly realised what this would mean. She might be forced to stay with Max alone. 'Is she that ill?' she protested, while ashamed that she could only think of herself.

'No,' the doctor replied ponderously, 'but for a while now she hasn't been too good. I think the strain of Miss Hartley's last illness took a lot out of her, but what she really needs is a change more than anything else.'

'Why not a short holiday? I could go with her.'

Dr Lewis shook his head at the strained eagerness in Selena's face. 'I don't believe that would be nearly so good. Max is going to pay for this, and Bronwen has already agreed and is grateful.'

When the doctor had gone Max glanced at Selena coldly but refused to indulge her obviously bursting indignation. 'My things are upstairs,' he said harshly. 'You can unpack for me. I have neither the time nor the inclination.'

So Bronwen was going to enjoy herself, and so was he. She was the one who was to suffer! He hadn't changed his mind about that, if the unforgiving glint in his eye was anything to go by. 'I-I'll think about it?' she stammered, on a note of weak defiance.

'Do as you're told!' he snapped, so savagely, she fled.

As she unpacked for him her hands shook as, despite his curt statement that he had no time to spare, Max sa on the end of his bed and watched her. Her sense of enraged frustration only increased as she tried to control it, especially as she sensed he was wholly aware of how she was feeling.

'I told Lewis you won't be working for him again,' he said sardonically.

'I saw him myself, yesterday,' she rejoined tersely.

'He knows it was only a temporary measure, anyway,' Max shrugged.

Selena decided not to argue. There were other jobs, but she needed time to think first. Pretending a casual indifference, she nodded.

'Is there a fire in the sitting-room?' Max enquired curtly, as she remained silent.

'Yes,' she replied.

'Good,' he smiled, his eyes roving over her closely.

His smile was like a tiger's. Selena had an uneasy feeling that if she made one wrong move he would pounce. Yet, in spite of such a warning, an inner agitation goaded her to ask sarcastically, 'Do you want me to run a bath?'

'A good idea,' he accepted her offer so readily she wished she had held her tongue. Her heart was misbehaving badly enough, having to handle his most intimate articles of clothing. She couldn't risk running into him, probably with little on, in the bathroom! Mutely shaking her head, she rushed past him, straight downstairs. There were some things he must do for himself!

She was busy getting Bronwen her supper when Max put his head around the kitchen door. 'I'll have my meal in the dining room,' he said, both his voice and eyes so coldly arrogant as to still any protest she was about to make.

By ten, she was almost worn out with rushing to and fro each time Max rang. He ate a good supper, but he demanded wine, then his soup reheated, then his steak a little better done. He would have his coffee in the sitting-room, he said, and while she was at it, the fire made up.

He stared with an indifference that made her blood boil as she hauled in a heavy hod of coal. She would liked to have thrown the whole lot over his head, but again her courage failed her. Every time she felt like exploding, the thought of her father and Babs and the baby, all destitute, haunted her.

'I'm going to bed,' she said at ten-thirty, adding morosely, 'You can't want anything more!'

'Only a little more civility,' he replied menacingly, making it quite clear he wasn't prepared to overlook her tartness for ever.

Wistfully, as his eyes narrowed on her flushed face, she gazed at the warm, glowing fire. He hadn't asked her to join him, which served to remind her of the uncomfortable weeks he had spent in the kitchen before he had recovered his memory. Hastily, her flush deepening in sudden pain, she withdrew.

In her room she glanced at the bed with a sinking heart as she recalled the awful lumps in the mattress. Only sleeping pills might guarantee any rest on that! The only alternative was perhaps a hot bath. Gathering up her toilet things, she decided she had plenty of time before Max came to bed. He was knee deep in papers.

She was so exhausted she must have dozed off in the bath, for when she awoke the water was quite cold. Silently cursing her own stupidity, she pulled on her robe without bothering to dry first and rushed back to her room. She was almost there, just passing Max's door when he emerged and they collided.

'Does it always take you an hour to get into bed?' he snapped.

'I must have dozed off in the bath,' she gasped, feeling still half asleep.

'Really?' His cynical eyebrows rose.

'You can be sure I won't risk it happening again.' Licking her suddenly dry lips, she tried to back away from him. He must have been on his way to his own bath, for like herself he wore only a short robe. It wa similar to the one he had worn at Lynton but shorter, and the sinewy muscles of his powerful thighs and legs seemed tense. The healthy outdoor tan he had acquired was continued down his broad chest, blending into the curling dark hair. Selena knew an overwhelming desire to slide her hand inside the front of his robe, as she had done once before, and touch him.

The wild, frantic beating of her heart warned her only just in time. 'Excuse me,' she choked, dropping the hand she had unconsciously raised.

'In a moment!' Swiftly Max grasped her shoulders as she spun, pulling her ruthlessly back to him again. Blatantly his eyes probed, seeming to take in every trembling inch of her before returning to linger on her mouth. 'Am I right in believing there's something wrong with your memory now? Have you forgotten an incident similar to this which happened a while ago? A poor shaking man holding you in his arms, meekly accepting your contemptuous rebuff when he dared kiss you?'

The shame she felt was too real to be admitted. Lowering her eyes over the agony she knew must be in them, she murmured with more composure than she felt. 'Would you rather I had encouraged you? If I'd led you on how would you be feeling now?'

'Extremely satisfied, I imagine,' he mocked smoothly, his hands slipping from her shoulders to pull her close to the throbbing heat of his body.

The wild clamour of her pulse increased as she saw the harsh light of desire suddenly flame in the dark glance that seared over her face. The wind provided light music in the background, emphasising how alone they were. She tried to speak, but her voice was shaking and unsteady like her limbs, and when her eyes widened to gaze at him imploringly, she grew giddy and lost in the fiery darkness of his.

The last time he had held her, anger to the edge of violence had made his arms brutally hurtful. Tonight the anger was still there, but in a more controlled form.

She was held tightly against him, her legs on fire from the touch of his hard thighs, while the same heat, sweeping upwards, threatened to consume her completely.

'You're still damp,' he murmured thickly, as he dropped his dark head to nuzzle her throat. His jaw tensed as his mouth trailed slowly up her cheek and his teeth bit gently into her ear lobe. His hands were possessively massaging her back and hips, emotively moulding her to him. She felt his legs part as she slumped helplessly against him, taking fully her soft weight.

'I want to kiss you,' he muttered savagely, with no pity for her gasping protest. Growing used to obeying mindlessly, she turned up her lips. When Max's mouth closed demandingly over them, all thought of resistance fled from her tormented mind. The sensual expertise of his mouth released a burning excitement in her, making her cling to him tightly, even as instinct warned her faintly of the danger she was in.

'Max!' she groaned, as his mouth parted her lips, then played with them softly. Of their own volition her hands crept under his robe to feel the hair-roughened skin scorching her fingers. She heard his breath rasp harshly, felt one of his hands sliding down her stomach. She heard her own brief gasp of fleeting pain before it returned to move over her back again.

When, with a hoarse mutter, he lifted her to carry her to her room, she didn't struggle. Her robe fell away as she was caught high in his arms. She was aware of his mouth on her bared breasts, but she was beyond thinking. Her senses felt drugged and she only breathed with difficulty. With a moan she turned her bruised mouth against his shoulder, lost in a whirling ache of desire.

The suddenness of her release came as a shock. When abruptly he dropped her on the bed, she hadn't expected to be rejected so coldly. He made no attempt to join her on the cotton cover but withdrew with a control she wasn't immediately capable of.

When he almost flung her from him she could only stare up at him in a daze of undisguised longing. 'Max,' she whispered, her blue eyes, still heavy from their shared passion, softly pleading, 'where are you going?'

'Not far, but go to sleep, Selena.' His face taut, he ignored her query. Briefly his gaze went over her, his dark eyes hooded. Even if she hadn't been almost blinded by tears it would have been difficult to see what lay in them.

Her body seemed on fire with an unbearable warmth. 'Please, Max!' she moaned, her one desire to be near him again, to be held closely. Not to have him staring from such a distance, as though he hated her.

Immediately he stepped back, his handsome face pale, but hardening with a strange determination. 'Now you know what I've felt like every time you rejected me,' he said harshly. 'When desire made me so I couldn't sleep at nights for wanting you. When I, poor fool, was stupid enough to imagine I was falling in love with you.'

'Max!' It seemed all she could do was utter his name. Frantically she levered herself on an elbow, while with a sob she tried to pull her robe tightly around her. Pride deserted her as she whimpered, 'I know I've fallen in love with you. I—I suppose I did try to hurt you, but I'll go down on my knees if only you would forgive me. I've already told you I'm sorry.'

As she began blindly to scramble off the bed, his hands reached out to thrust her none too gently back again. 'I heard,' he sneered, 'but I'm not looking for any further displays of remorse. I'm not interested in how you feel, Selena, but I shouldn't worry over much, if I were you. You'll probably feel quite differently by morning.'

The door slammed behind him and she lay still, moaning softly with shock against her pillows. She hoped feverishly that she would feel better in the morning, but at the moment she was too tortured and full of distress even to find release in tears.

When daylight did arrive, she was surprised to discover Max's advice did contain at least some germ of truth. Nothing seemed to matter so much any more. She felt beautifully numb.

Even so, that didn't prevent her heart pounding as she carried his breakfast into the dining room, nor the painful despair that arose in her breast as she saw Max's face was as cold as the weather. He merely glanced up briefly from the pile of papers he was still absorbing and asked her to pour his coffee.

Taking no notice of her pale, strained face, he said curtly, 'This comes from being out of circulation for so long. I've arranged for one of the secretaries to come and help. For a start she can get this little lot sorted out. She'll need lunch, though.'

Selena had been about to offer impulsively to help with his correspondence herself, but managed to stop herself in time. She had enough to do and she wouldn't know where to start. Besides, hadn't she had enough of Max's snapping and snarling to last her the rest of her life!

Still, her heart ached fiercely with what she reluctantly recognised as jealousy as she let in an extremely attractive, brown-eyed girl an hour later. Miss Shore stared at Selena so curiously it took Selena all her time to smile politely and take her through to Max.

Max had the dining room table strewn with papers and though he glanced up impatiently he greeted Miss Shore civilly enough. When Selena returned with their coffee she found them both hard at work.

'Oh, Selena?' Max smiled. 'Norma and I will just have a working lunch here, so we don't have to stop, and perhaps a cup of tea before she leaves to return to the hotel this evening.'

Which was one way of preventing people knowing he didn't eat with his girl-friend, Selena supposed, bitter rage consuming her as she compared the graciousness of his manner towards her when others were present with what she was forced to put up with when they were alone.

In one way she was relieved that he was busy, and even more so when, after tea, he departed with Miss Shore and didn't return until after midnight. It was a routine he followed without much deviation during the next few days. He worked with Miss Shore in the mornings and afternoons at Moor Edge, then spent the evenings with his team at the hotel. As his temper didn't improve much Selena knew she ought to be glad when he was gone for even a few hours, yet somehow she missed him intolerably. That she was kept busy herself, cooking meals and getting Bronwen's wardrobe ready for her stay in the convalescent home, enabled her to ignore to some extent the true agony she realised she would suffer when Max was gone for good.

'Bronwen is leaving the day after tomorrow,' she reminded him one morning as she carried in his breakfast.

'On Friday,' he agreed levelly, glancing narrowly at Selena as he usually did. 'What about it?'

Wondering if he was being deliberately obtuse, she took a deep breath. 'We can't stay here alone!'

'Really?' His eyebrows rose dryly. 'No one's going to harm us.'

Selena felt her face grow bright red, although she managed to control the worst of her temper. 'You may enjoy poking fun at me, Max, but I won't do it. You treat me like dirt—perhaps I deserve it, but I won't stay with you alone.'

Again his brows rose smoothly. 'What do you suggest, then? Shall I ask Miss Shore to move in? Somehow I don't think she'd be so adverse to sharing my bed.'

How dared he emphasise that! Selena encouraged her rage to subdue the cold dismay she felt. She would have to be blind to miss the adoring glances Norma Shore showered on Max, or the deliberate calculation in his eyes as he occasionally returned them.

'I don't think that's a good idea, either,' Selena replied tersely, between her teeth, 'and, seeing how much wine she's capable of consuming with her lunch, it would probably cost you a fortune.'

'There might be worse ways of spending my money,' he grinned wickedly.

Which drove Selena to betray what little dignity she seemed to have left by actually stamping her foot. 'Never say I didn't warn you!' she shouted, beating a hasty retreat before he could see the hot tears of defeat streaming down her cheeks.

On Friday morning at eleven a taxi arrived for Bronwen, complete with a friend from the village who was going to accompany her on her journey. Selena couldn't help feeling a little hurt as she had offered to go with Bronwen herself and been turned down.

'I've known Bella all my life,' Bronwen explained again, with a quick, almost furtive glance at Max, who was helping to see her off. 'But I'll be delighted to see you and Mr—Max, any time after your—your——'

'Yes?' Selena prompted, a puzzled frown on her face as she waited for Bronwen to finish. She wasn't usually at loss for words.

'I mean whenever you can get away,' Bronwen said hastily, as she climbed in the taxi.

'Of course I'll come.' Selena didn't include Max. 'Just as soon as you've got settled in I'll be there.' She kissed Bronwen warmly goodbye. 'Just get well soon.'

Selena waved until the taxi was out of sight while she groped blindly for the best way out of the frightening situation Bronwen's departure had created. When she turned it was to find Max still behind her, watching her enigmatically.

'Hasn't Miss Shore arrived yet?' she asked blankly. She had been so busy calming an excited Bronwen all morning, she hadn't noticed.

'She isn't coming today,' Max replied rather tersely, his eyes never leaving her.

'Oh.' Selena didn't know what else to say.

'Nor again,' Max muttered, 'for several weeks. I don't want her interrupting my honeymoon.'

'Your—honeymoon!'

'Don't sound so shocked,' he drawled, taking in her white face. 'A man usually has one after he marries, but until I finish my last film I won't be able to get away. That's why I thought here. It's as good a place as any.'

'I see.' Feeling ill and more shaken than she would ever have believed, Selena looked at him, numb misery in her eyes. So that was what he had been doing in London? He must have seen someone there, a girl whom he loved. Pain made her tremble as she whispered, 'You never mentioned anything before.'

'No.' Suddenly, his face carved in dark, haggard lines, his indifference dropped from him like a cloak as he grasped her wrist. 'Let's go inside, darling. I believe I have some explaining to do.'

It wasn't until after he had very carefully closed the door behind them and bundled her into the sitting-room that she took in exactly what he said.

'You have some explaining to do?' she asked breathlessly.

'Yes.' His voice unusually constricted, Max turned to grasp her shoulders, in a manner which suggested he would never let her go. His eyes were dark, full of flames which threatened to leap out and burn her. She tried to find something to ease his obvious torment, but found she couldn't speak. If she had, she doubted he would have heard. All his cool contempt was gone, but she loved him so much she could scarcely bear to see the burning agony that replaced it.

'What is it you want to say?' she managed at last.

'My love,' he muttered thickly, 'I'm trying to explain that you're the girl I want to marry. No,' his voice was harsher but more distinct, 'you're the girl I'm going to marry, later this afternoon, in Exeter. I was there as well as in London last week, making the necessary arrangements. You might curse me for being so high-handed, but I didn't think there was any other way.'

Her heart thudded in her throat, her eyes widened in stunned astonishment as she stared back at him. 'But you hate me!' she gasped. 'You couldn't forgive me for what I did.'

With a groan, as if he couldn't bear her bewildered unhappiness a moment longer, Max drew her to him, crushing her tear-wet face against his shoulder. 'I tried to hate you, my darling,' he amended dryly, 'but it never got off the ground. I love you and want to marry you so much, and we don't have a lot of time.'

'You must have been very sure of me,' she whispered bleakly.

'The only thing I was sure of,' he said harshly, 'was our reactions. You must have felt the force of the attraction we have for each other. I tried to ignore it, but I couldn't pretend it didn't exist. Even when I was away from you, I couldn't forget how soft your skin was when I touched it. The need to see you constantly was like an ache. I couldn't bear to be away from you. I felt I was being slowly driven crazy and unable to do a thing about it.'

'Oh, darling!' Selena half swallowed before the leashed passion in his voice, unable to hide her own feelings. Blindly she raised her hot face, whispering tremulously of her love for him as his mouth descended savagely on her trembling lips. As he lifted her to bring her down across his knees on the wide settee beside the fire, her whole being seemed to throb beneath the sensuous, demanding passion of his kiss. As he slowly raised his head, the thought of marrying him was still too hazy to be truly believable. Yet even to let the idea flicker through her mind brought a quivering delight—and a rather apprehensive excitement.

He smoothed the heavy hair from off her flushed cheeks, his mouth tender. 'You haven't said yes,' he reminded her softly.

She managed to smile faintly, lost on the depth of his compelling gaze. 'You didn't ask me. You just told me.'

Max seemed to have no desire at the moment to return her smile, and the hand caressing her face went curiously still. 'Well, I'm asking you now.'

A faint frown flickered over her smooth brow. 'I always vowed I'd never marry a man like you.'

'Why?' he exclaimed tersely.

'Oh, the usual reasons,' she tried to reply lightly. 'Too many divorces in the acting profession, too much infidelity.'

'I wasn't even aware you knew what that word meant,' he teased.

'I'm not a child, Max!' In her indignation, she struggled to sit up, but he wouldn't allow it. He merely crushed her closer, as though he couldn't bear to have her leave his arms.

'No,' his mouth sobered as it touched her cheek. 'I suppose you feel as you do because of your parents, but when you consider the pressures it's perhaps understandable. Plenty of people in my profession, as you call it, do have stable and very loving marriages. You only have to look around.'

A sudden thought struck Selena, making her quiver. Uncertainly she raised her eyes to his face. 'You once told me you'd been married but that your wife had died. But perhaps you were divorced? I don't mean to pry darling,' she whispered, as his face went grim.

'You aren't prying,' he shook his head. 'I wasn't going to marry you without telling you, but I thought you might know.'

'Only what you told me before,' she murmured.

'There's not much more to tell,' he said slowly, his grey eyes suddenly bleak. 'She was a girl who was born in the same village as me. I was twenty-four when I discovered her in London, eleven years ago. She was ill and destitute. Her parents were dead and she was all alone and suffering from a rare blood disease. She badly needed someone to look after her, but, to this day, I'm not really sure why I married her. My parents were wealthy. I'd always been cushioned from the harsher realities of life and I think I resented it. When this girl came along I was struggling to get away from them and I suppose I saw this as another score against parental authority. Or possibly I imagined myself as a kind of modern knight, rescuing a fair maiden in distress.'

Briefly he paused, his voice deepening. 'She only lived six months after we were married and most of the time she was in hospital. She died there, no one could have saved her.'

'Were you very sad when she died?' Selena asked gently, after a moment's silence, her eyes full of compassion.

'No,' Max said firmly, 'no one could have been sad to have seen such suffering ended, but I had regrets.'

'What sort of regrets?' Selena wondered softly.

'I'm not sure.' Again she sensed he was trying to be completely honest. 'Every time I think of it, which I admit isn't often, I find myself wondering what Carol got out of it, rather than myself. Those six months certainly helped me grow up. It also made me realise how necessary it was to have real feelings for someone before entering into marriage. If Carol had lived, I began to understand what our life might have been like without love to help carry us through.'

Gazing at him with an adoration she no longer made any attempt to hide, Selena put a hand gently to his cheek. 'It was such a wonderful thing to do that I'm sure you'd have found the courage.'

'But I can't be sure,' he exclaimed curtly, 'and it doesn't help that I'll never know. It did make me determined, however, that I'd never ask another girl to marry me unless I really meant it, and I never thought that day would come until I met you.'

'You—you never married again?'

'No.' A glint in his eye teasing her, he shook his head.

'But that doesn't mean I've lived entirely without women. I can only say I've never looked at anyone else since I met you. I might have tried to,' his firm mouth curved ironically, 'but they didn't do a thing for me when all I could see, night and day, was a pair of beautiful blue eyes.'

'Ours wasn't a very auspicious meeting.' Selena sensed that his first marriage had been a greater ordeal than he said, and she would be wiser to talk of other things. Gently she teased him back, 'I'm surprised you ever spared me another thought!'

'So am I, my dear.' In mock severity he gazed down on her. 'Not only did I fracture my wrist but my heart suffered irreparable damage. I don't know yet how I came to grab you and kiss you the way I did. You upset my life so much that for a long time I put it down to the work of the devil.'

'Really?' Selena's grin widened, then faded, as their eyes met. 'I felt the same,' she confessed, 'and I probably understood it less.'

'Just as long as you understand that,' he groaned thickly, claiming her lips with a thoroughness which left them both reeling with mutual desire. 'Oh, darling!' he laid her flatly on the settee, pressing himself gently over her as he began undoing the buttons on her blouse. When she feebly protested, he muttered hoarsely, 'You'd have been taking it off yourself to get ready for our wedding, wouldn't you?'

Weakly she gave in as his kisses aroused a burning excitement that swept away all her resistance.

Hoarsely he began muttering against her warm throat. 'I tried hard to forget you, put you out of my mind, but I failed. Why do you think I went to Pearl's party if it wasn't in the hope of meeting you again? I had this vague notion that you might be there. Then you had to make me furious by apparently having no intention of confessing you'd ever seen me before. I took you to my flat because I was determined to find out the truth for myself. When I kissed you I knew I need seek no further proof. I told myself I had to have you, whatever the cost!'

He paused, as if he found it difficult to go on, while his hands explored the rounded contours of her body until her lips parted and she moaned with tormented delight.

His mouth coming back to her cheek, he murmured fiercely, 'Yes, you deserve to suffer! When you were so unfriendly, in London, I decided wrongly that you needed time. I offered you a job, where I knew we could be together and was livid when you turned it down. I still couldn't believe you wanted nothing to do with me, so I tried a little blackmail regarding Pearl and decided a weekend at Lynton would finalise matters.'

'You also tried to persuade me with a fur coat and a fabulous dinner,' she reminded him reproachfully. 'I hated that.'

'I was in a hurry, and desperate!' Max returned sulkily. His arms tightened as his eyes hardened with something like anger. 'I wonder you dare mention that when I recall how I overheard you on the telephone, when I came to collect you for Lynton. You were promising yourself to another man. I almost went mad! I told myself I was going to be first.'

'Oh, Max!' she gasped, breathless from his weight on her. 'That was Ronald, the writer I worked for! I should have been working for him instead of going to Lynton. I promised to stay all night, if necessary, only to finish his book. He has a housekeeper, anyway, who watches over him like a hawk. Actually he hasn't been in touch since I spoke to him that day. He's doing something abroad.'

'Oh, God,' Max groaned, 'if only I'd known! It was partly because I imagined you were about to start having an affair with him that I tried to persuade you to come to America. Once I had you there I thought you'd be quite safe from this other man. When all my persuasions failed I didn't know what to do. I would have asked you to marry me, but I didn't think you loved me, and my pride couldn't face your possible ridicule. I think I went quietly berserk. When I came to your room, that night at Lynton, I meant to make love to you. Whatever else happened I was going to have you.'

'But you didn't,' Selena whispered, as his breath rasped.

'I discovered, at the last moment, that I couldn't treat you like that,' he said huskily against her hot face. 'All the same, I couldn't get my mind completely untwisted. I decided you should at least share my suffering. That's why I wrote that note.'

'When I read it I did suffer,' she recalled bleakly.

'Darling, don't!' His voice thick with remorse, Max pressed hot kisses on her trembling lips, before he continued darkly, 'I hadn't been in the States five minutes before I knew I couldn't live without you. I wanted you for my wife, to be able to look after you, to cherish you, to be able to love you in every possible way. I wound up my business commitments, actually,' he confessed, 'I left most of it undone. I told Deirdre and Kit I was getting a licence and marrying you, that we would be away for several weeks on our honeymoon. I swore them to secrecy because I couldn't be absolutely sure you'd say yes. You still haven't,' he added, but in a tone that made her suspect he wouldn't listen if she said no.

'Would you let me refuse?' she smiled, adding thoughtfully, when he smiled tautly back and shook his head, 'So that must have been why no one appeared to miss you?'

'I suppose so,' he replied. 'I made all the arrangements and was on my way here, a licence in my pocket, along with other things. That's why I asked about my jacket. In one of the pockets I had two very nice rings.'

'Oh, Max,' Selena's small face was pale, 'if only I'd known! I thought you had—had owned and rejected me,' she stammered, 'and my life was finished. I believed you were here only to study the countryside, because of your film. I never imagined it would be so long before you recovered your memory. When time went on I grew almost frantic. I loved you so much and I didn't know what to do. I should have told you, though, not left you to find out the way you did. Then you were so angry,' she faltered. 'I know I deserved it, but I was so miserable.'

'Darling, don't,' he muttered, as if the memory of that day haunted him too. 'It was a peculiar experience, having anything rushing back at me without warning, some things sooner than others. It took me time, I'll admit, to get my balance. I controlled everything instinctively, I think, while Pearl was there. Then it was as though a dam burst in my head. All I could immediately comprehend was that you'd known and never told me. You'd let me suffer and go on suffering. It suggested you hated rather than loved me, and I really did feel savage about that.'

Selena nodded to let him see she accepted this, but her eyes filled with painful tears. 'When you went on being savage, I thought you hated me!'

'I had to pretend to,' he said fiercely. 'It was either that or make love to you completely, and I needed time to get another licence and make other, necessary arrangements. I wasn't even sure until the other night that you cared for me, which didn't improve my temper.'

As those moments in her bedroom came back with a rush, Selena felt herself consumed by a great longing. 'I've loved you for a long time,' she whispered, her arms clinging to him feverishly.

'Well, never hide it again,' Max said menacingly. 'It's been a struggle, these last two days, holding myself back, since I discovered that interesting fact. However,' he relented, with what she could only consider a look of smug satisfaction, 'I've got everything fixed so we should have at least a week alone here together before I have to begin work again. After I finish this film we'll have a proper honeymoon, then we'll settle at Lynton, where I hope to write and raise a family. With your help,' he added softly, his eyes glinting.

The pulsing warmth in her body quickly affected her face, which she tried to hide against him. 'What will your team think when they hear of you getting married?'

She felt his wry smile against the top of her head. 'I don't think any of them could have mistaken the way I was looking at you the other night. Nor my reactions when I discovered you'd disappeared with Mr Pleasure. You'll find,' he teased dryly, 'that they'll be very pleased someone has tamed me at last. And by the way, darling, I told your father the news in London, and we can tell your mother later.'

Because, blissfully, there seemed little left to say, certainly nothing that wouldn't keep, Selena pulled his dark head down and began kissing him again. Just for a moment his arms tightened, as if he was prepared to forget everything but the inviting curve of her mouth and the surrendering softness of her slender body.

Then suddenly she found herself standing on her feet, and, as she gazed at him in hurt astonishment, he exclaimed, 'Have you forgotten we're getting married in just over an hour's time, young lady, and you haven't even got your make-up on?' His teasing smile half hid the smouldering longing in his eyes. 'I'm doing my best to make an honest woman of you, but you aren't even trying to help me.'

'Oh, Max!' As their eyes met Selena felt her whole being dissolve in an anticipatory glow. 'I wouldn't miss marrying you for the world. I wouldn't exchange you for it, either, I love you.'

'Just so long as you're still saying that in fifty years time,' he threatened as, with a swift kiss, he took her hand and together they went upstairs to prepare for their wedding.

The Mills & Boon Rose is the Rose of Romance

Every month there are ten new titles to choose from — ten new
stories about people falling in love, people you want to read
about, people in exciting, far-away places. Choose Mills & Boon.
It's your way of relaxing.

August's titles are:

COLLISION by *Margaret Pargeter*
After the heartless way Max Heger had treated her, Selena wanted
to be revenged on him. But things didn't work out as she had
planned.

DARK REMEMBRANCE by *Daphne Clair*
Could Raina marry Logan Thorne a year after her husband Perry's
death, when she knew that Perry would always come first with her?

AN APPLE FROM EVE by *Betty Neels*
Doctor Tane van Diederijk and his fiancée were always cropping
up in Euphemia's life. If only she could see the back of both of
them?

COPPER LAKE by *Kay Thorpe*
Everything was conspiring to get Toni engaged to Sean. But she
was in love with his brother Rafe — who had the worst possible
opinion of her!

INVISIBLE WIFE by *Jane Arbor*
Vicente Massimo blamed Tania for his brother's death. So how
was it that Tania soon found herself blackmailed into marrying him?

BACHELOR'S WIFE by *Jessica Steele*
Penny's marriage to Nash Devereux had been a ' paper ' one. So
why did Nash want a reconciliation just when Penny wanted to
marry Trevor?

CASTLE IN SPAIN by *Margaret Rome*
Did Birdie love the lordly Vulcan, Conde de la Conquista de Retz
— who wanted to marry her — or did she fear him?

KING OF CULLA by *Sally Wentworth*
After the death of her sister, Marnie wanted to be left alone.
But the forceful Ewan McNeill didn't seem to get the message!

ALWAYS THE BOSS by *Victoria Gordon*
The formidable Conan Garth was wrong in every opinion he held
of Dinah — but could she ever make him see it?

CONFIRMED BACHELOR by *Roberta Leigh*
Bradley Dexter was everything Robyn disliked. But now that she
could give him a well-deserved lesson, fate was playing tricks on
her!

If you have difficulty in obtaining any of these books from your
local paperback retailer, write to:

Mills & Boon Reader Service
P.O. Box 236, Thornton Road, Croydon, Surrey, CR9 3RU.
Available August 1981

ROMANCE

Variety is the spice of romance

Each month, Mills & Boon publish new romances. New stories about people falling in love. A world of variety in romance – from the best writers in the romantic world. Choose from these titles in September.

THE LION OF LA ROCHE   Yvonne Whittal
SATAN'S MASTER   Carole Mortimer
ILLUSION   Charlotte Lamb
SUBSTITUTE BRIDE   Margaret Pargeter
UNTOUCHED WIFE   Rachel Lindsay
INNOCENT OBSESSION   Anne Mather
WITCHING HOUR   Sara Craven
HILLS OF AMETHYST   Mary Moore
PASSIONATE STRANGER   Flora Kidd
MACLEAN'S WOMAN   Ann Cooper

On sale where you buy paperbacks. If you require further information or have any difficulty obtaining them, write to: Mills & Boon Reader Service, PO Box 236, Thornton Road, Croydon, Surrey CR9 3RU, England.

Mills & Boon
the rose of romance

Mills & Boon
Best Seller Romances

The very best of Mills & Boon Romances

brought back for those of you who missed

them when they were first published.

In August
we bring back the following four
great romantic titles.

STORMY HAVEN
by Rosalind Brett

When Melanie came to the island of Mindoa in the Indian Ocean she was little more than a schoolgirl; when she left, only eight months later, she had grown into a woman. Her scheming cousin Elfrida, Ramon Perez and the masterful Stephen Brent had all played their parts in this transformation.

BOSS MAN FROM OGALLALA
by Janet Dailey

Casey knew she was perfectly capable of running her father's ranch for him while he was in hospital. It was *only* because she was a girl that Flint McCallister had been brought in to do the job. So what with one thing and another, there was hardly a warm welcome waiting for the new boss!

DARK CASTLE
by Anne Mather

What Julie had once felt for Jonas Hunter was now past history and she had made every effort to keep it so. But now she found herself travelling to Scotland to make contact with him again. Could she manage to remain on purely business terms with the man who had meant so much to her and whose attraction for her had increased rather than lessened?

THE GIRL AT DANES' DYKE
by Margaret Rome

'Women aren't welcome at Danes' Dyke,' the inscrutable Thor Halden told Raine; nevertheless circumstances forced him to take her under his roof for a time, and to persuade her to masquerade as his wife. It was a difficult enough situation for Raine, even before she found herself falling in love with him. Would she ever be able to make him trust her?

If you have difficulty in obtaining any of these books through your local paperback retailer, write to:

Mills & Boon Reader Service
P.O. Box 236, Thornton Road, Croydon, Surrey, CR9 3RU.